LITTLE GUTS

LITTLE GUTS

LITTLE GUTS

THE GUTS

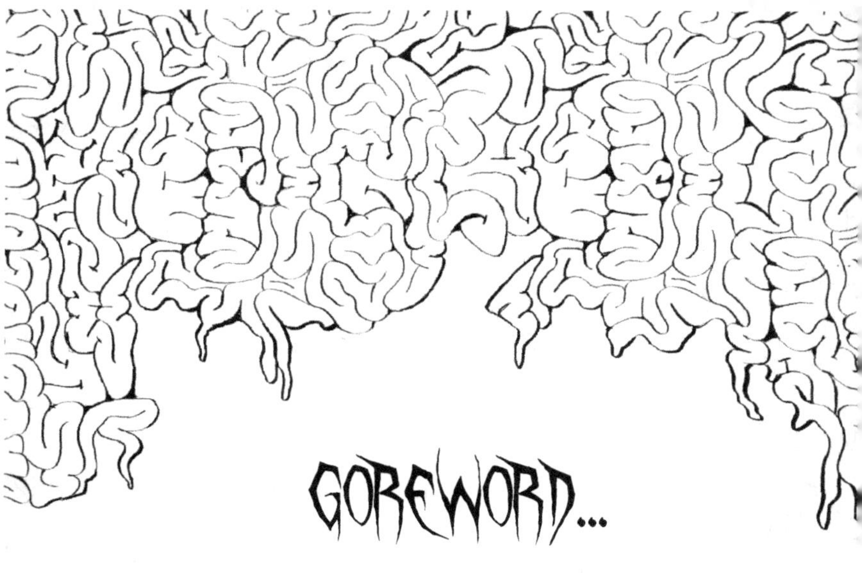

GOREWORD...

Filth and fun go together like peas in a pod.

Each generation of horror, from films to toys and stories, has its fair share of goop, grime and guts. There's something that scratches an itch in this that I can't find elsewhere, something primal about squishing your hands in a pile of raw meat, or feeling the wet sand between your toes…it's gratifying. I am an animal in need of enrichment, delighted by abundance.

Even outside of horror, filth is *entertainment.* Pimple popping, surgery footage, countless hours of oddly satisfying wet weird slime are but a click away. Any and every fetish you could think of, and some you couldn't.

There's a commonality to guts within every human being, to know we are all just piles of mushy organs and wet bones wandering around and making the best of it.

It's with this sentiment *Little Guts* was put together: to bring together authors who are rolling in the pigsty with me, to explore the depths and heights of the grotesque while remaining silly.

I'd like to thank each and every one of them for pouring their guts out to me, for making me laugh and retch and cry. To Chris and Little Ghosts for their continued love and dedication to championing horror, especially the lil guys.

With love,
LG (Lor Gislason)

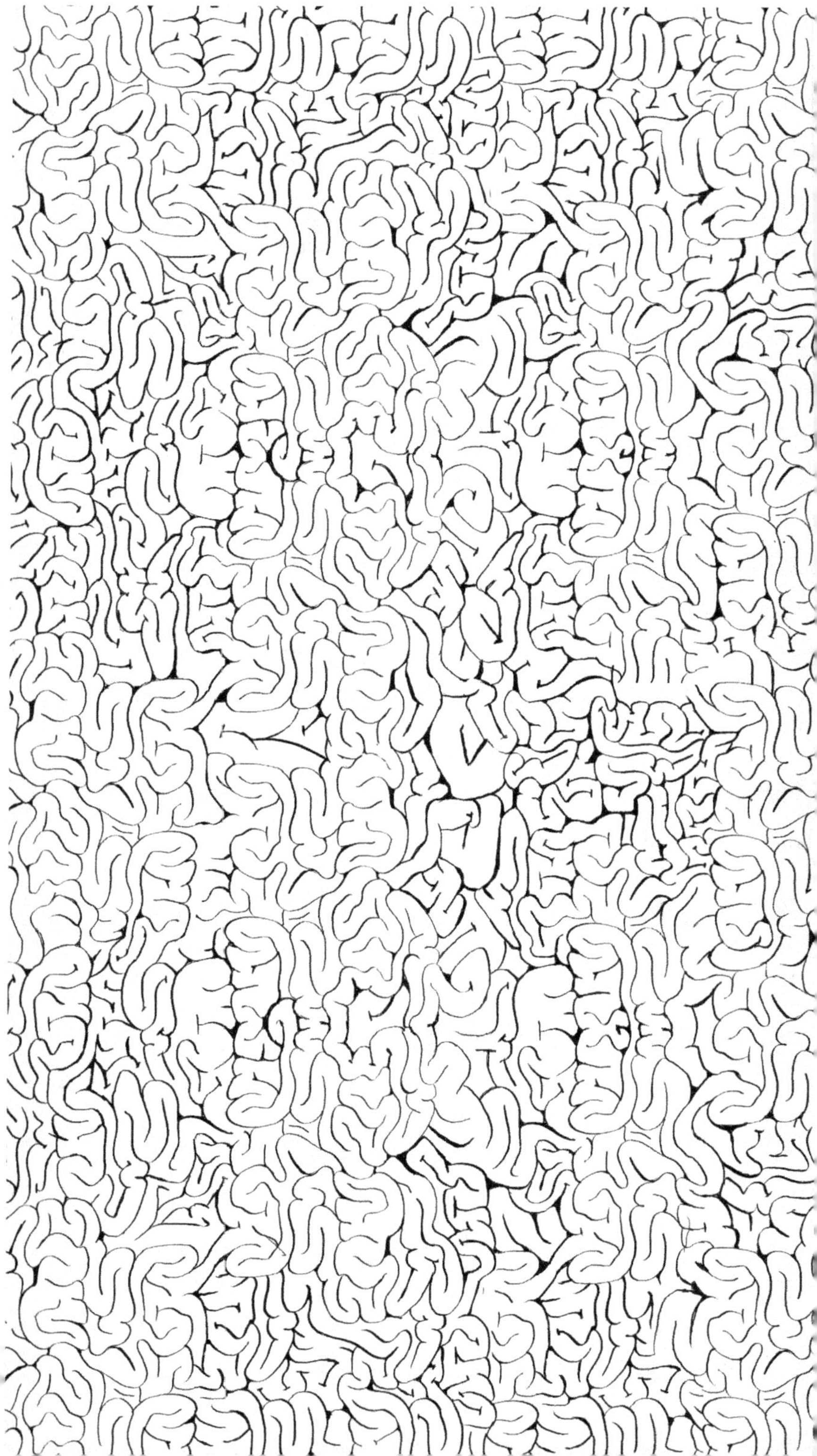

GUTS FOR GLORY
KEEGAN HUGHES

Good evening to all of those just tuning in—it's Hockey Night in New Canada!

We've got one hell of a bout lined up tonight, Rick. The Timmins Thrashers are set to take on the Saguenay Nordiques in a grudge match to end all grudge matches.

That's right, Guy. You could feel the animosity as soon as the teams exited their dressing rooms. The rivalry between them has reached a new level, especially after their last meeting. Back in February, the Nordiques pulled off a decisive victory—winning 5-2—but their captain, Francois Tremblay, left the game early with two broken legs. You can expect some sort of response from his team tonight.

Yeah, Weatherspoon got him good. The Thrashers' hulking winger took a run at Tremblay, and blew him right off his feet with a hip check. He must've been five feet in the air! It didn't help that Weatherspoon took a whack at him as soon as he was on the ice, either.

The resulting bench brawl was a memorable one, too! The ice crew had one hell of a time collecting all the scattered teeth.

Love a good beatdown! Especially when they pull some rookies into the action. You can always count on a greenhorn to let their guard down. That's where blood can really get spilled.

Speaking of rookies; tonight marks the debut of the Thrashers' newest winger wearing number 56: Brandon Connelly! He's a local boy, and spent some time playing in the minors. Strong on the puck, likes to shoot, but hasn't really shown any killer instinct. We'll see what being in the spotlight does to him.

Looks like we're about to get started here, Rick. Timmins versus Saguenay! The puck is about to drop!

Coming off of the face-off, the Nordiques are out for blood! Lavoie takes a swing at Weatherspoon and gets him clean in the mouth with the shaft of his stick.

Ouch! Weatherspoon is down! Would you look at the waterfall that used to be his mouth?

Play continues as the Thrashers move the puck up ice. Gardiner crosses the blue line unimpeded, and looks to his right. Weatherspoon isn't there, as he's still collecting his teeth.

You have to wonder what he's thinking, going back for his pearly-whites. I guess he's worried that soon there won't be any left! Not many players still sport a full set, that's for sure!

Gardiner drops the puck back for the captain, Thompson, who winds up for a heavy slap shot! That shot whips wide, and ends up in the corner. Weatherspoon is back in the play, skating hard to the boards. Nordiques defenceman Belanger is there, looking for his pound of flesh.

Watch out! OH! Belanger chops down on Weatherspoon's shoulder hard. You could hear the blade of the stick hit bone from here! Seems like his arm is still attached to him, though.

That can't feel good, Guy. A couple more whacks, and he'll be a limb short! For now, Weatherspoon powers through. He's handling the puck with one hand on his stick. He pushes it around the bend, and out to the blue line.

Warner is there to pick it up, and he stick-handles to the middle of the ice. He's got an open lane, and is now skating it towards the net. Drags it to the left and—

HOLY MACKINAW! Nordiques centre LeGuerrier runs him straight through with his stick! Talk about spearing! He's been skewered!

Warner is doubled over between the circles, grasping at the stick that's punctured him. Doesn't look like he'll be grasping for long, though, as LeGuerrier is trying to yank his stick free.

One, two, and—ooooooooh! Three will do it! Would you look at that spray! His stick is free of Warner's midsection—along with a significant length of Warner's intestines! It's like a butcher shop on sausage day! And it seems like he had spaghetti for dinner.

LeGuerrier now has a couple kills on his stat sheet. A player to keep an eye on for sure.

Guess Warner didn't read the scouting report tonight! He's not getting back up.

The puck skitters back out over the blue line, and now the Nordiques are pushing the play. Piquette, with Weatherspoon's blood still on his stick, dumps the puck in deep and heads off for a change. Timmins follows suit, although they're currently short a player.

And they will be until someone can manage to drag Warner off the ice. He was trying for a second there, but seems to have run out of gas!

The Timmins defensive duo of Breckenridge and Horner are out now, and you can be sure that they'll be looking for redemption. For now, Horner picks up the puck and looks for the outlet pass. He might not have time, though, as Thiel skates in with a head full of steam. Horner opts to send it across the ice to Breckenridge to buy a few seconds. Breckenridge sees Poirier near centre ice and fires it up the boards.

Poirier has the puck, but is quickly pressured by the Nordiques defence. He's gonna think twice before skating it up the middle, though.

He stops up at the blue line and looks for a pass. Merriweather is slow to catch up, but that doesn't seem to matter. Horner has grabbed Thiel—and it looks like there's going to be a fight!

Here we go! Both players have dropped their gloves, and are now circling each other. Horner knew what he was going to do from the moment he stepped off the bench. Thiel is looking a little shaky, but he'll take the ticket. Horner lunges in and grabs Thiel's jersey, yanking him toward the ice. Thiel is taken a little off balance, but he's still on both feet. Thiel swings, but only gets Horner's shoulder. And that's all the room Horner needs! He feeds Thiel a quick punch to the chin, and just keeps going! What is that, four, no—five solid punches! Thiel has to be feeling that sweet chin music.

Horner isn't showing any signs of backing off, and Thiel is looking less than steady! He tosses a half-hearted punch, but misses the mark again. This fight is all Horner!

There's another series of punches from Horner! He's relentless! Thiel's face is starting to look like the business end of a meat grinder. Where did his nose go? I think it's totally collapsed into his face!

You could be right, Guy! And with that—Thiel is down! But Horner isn't letting up! He's grabbed the front of Thiel's jersey with both hands, and is pounding his head into the ice!

Every smack of his skull leaves behind a wet, red dot! Reminds me of Bingo night down at the Legion! If he keeps this up, Thiel won't just be missing his nose—he'll be missing the majority of his head!

The ref has finally blown the play dead—we'll have a short break to let the cleaning crew take care of this. That's a lot of grey matter on the ice, Guy.

Ah, I love the cleaning crew. They do their job so efficiently, and there's nothing quite like a fresh sheet of ice! You can tell they take great pride in what they do.

We'll be back in just a moment.

…

Brandon Connolly barely made it through the first period. A huge hit in the corner took him off his feet and left his ears ringing, but he got up and kept on going. No blood, no missing limbs, no problem. His legs hadn't stopped shaking since lining up for the mandatory participation of the national anthem. And now, after seeing what happened to Warner, he was going to be extra careful. Brandon had seen people lose teeth, wads of hair, and limbs. One of his earliest memories was watching some poor sap on the visiting Whalers get his throat ripped open. He didn't think it was possible for the ice to be so red. But getting disembowelled in the middle of the ice? In front of so many people? That was brutal.

Going into the second period, he decided that playing it safe was probably the best option. He just had to remember what his dad used to tell him: *Keep your head up, and your stick on the ice.* At this point, keep your head on seemed more appropriate. Although, his dad played hockey before Canada became New Canada. Sure, they revelled in the sport's violence back then too, but nobody was going out there with the goal of hacking someone's leg off below the knee. Plus, they still wore protective gear.

The game was extra brutal now—not many players made it through a whole season. But if you could put together a good string of games, the league would take care of you. Not on the ice, of course, but by getting your family some more fresh food. A day out of the mines. Maybe a can of beer or two.

That's why Brandon had to put on a good show tonight. Stick to the fundamentals, keep it simple. Shoot the puck in deep, forecheck hard, try to hurt someone. Try to avoid a fight—just because his mom would hate that. *Especially* after that guy on the Nordiques got brained. Brandon started to wonder how Coach Skinner was going to deploy the fourth line in the second. The Thrashers were down a couple goals, and needed their stars to pick up the pace. Horton was a good option, but his linemate, Weatherspoon—or Spooner, as the boys called him—was having a tough night. Kinda hard to shoot and pass with part of your arm missing.

Spooner's night got even worse as the puck dropped to start the second. Lavoie, still out for blood, took another whack at his injured arm. The blade of Lavoie's stick found purchase in the separation between shoulder and torso, and stayed there. Brandon watched from the bench as Spooner tried to tug away. Every inch he twisted from Lavoie was an inch of flesh the blade shredded. At this point, the bone was entirely free of the socket. Tendons and veins were severed, and the ones that held on were stretched thin. With a quick jerk of his stick, Lavoie relieved Weatherspoon of his dangling appendage—the bloodied limb hit the ice with a wet slap.

As his stump sprayed blood onto the nearby players, all Weatherspoon could do was stare helplessly at the empty space his massive arm used to occupy. By the time he realized what had happened, the play was halfway across the ice. Holding his stick with one hand, he clumsily skated after Lavoie. Seeing the hulking winger continue to skate after losing his arm, Brandon wondered if he could do the same. Could he keep his wits about him and keep on throwing hits while actively bleeding out?

Weatherspoon never caught up to Lavoie, and eventually came back to the bench for a line change. The trainer took him aside, and used some foam sealant to staunch the bleeding. With that, Spooner wouldn't bleed out. But he definitely wouldn't be the same player after tonight.

As Line Two took to the ice, Brandon felt the cold grip of nerves deep in the pit of his stomach. A couple more forty-five-second shifts, and he'd be out there. Expected to make a difference. Back in the juniors, he could score. He did it often. But the other players tended to be a lot smaller, and way less bloodthirsty. Something about the huge crowds at Hockey Night games really got people riled up—both on and off the ice. The crowd expected to see some carnage, and the players obliged. Scoring goals almost seemed secondary; a relic from the past, grandfathered in to give some structure to the bloodsport-on-ice.

Suddenly, Coach Skinner was shouting. The rest of the boys on the bench were yelling, too. Some were red in the face, absolutely furious. Others, green. Brandon had been too lost in thought, too nervous. He missed something big.

Anderson, on the third line, was curled up in a ball in the middle of the ice. Arms rigid, legs crossed. Something oblong rolling across the ice in a wide arc, leaving a thin trail of red behind. Now the blood was starting to pool around Anderson's waist. Oh, no.

"Connolly!"

Brandon's head whipped around to look at Coach Skinner. Anderson was playing on the right wing, which meant that his third line position was now open. Brandon would be heading out onto the ice a little earlier than expected.

As they got ready for for the face-off, Brandon looked at his linemates: On the left was Gord Bear. A vet. Absolutely covered in scars, but still kicking. Perera was playing centre. He was pretty new to the league, but seemed to fit in pretty well. Brandon heard that he bit someone's ear off during a scrum, Tyson style. It was good to have him out there, as he'd take most of the attention if things got hairy.

The ref skated up with the puck, ready to drop it. Brandon hunkered down and put his stick on the ice. Looking ahead, he saw that the opposing winger was missing his left eye. He hadn't even bothered to get a prosthetic. All that remained was an infected, fleshy well. A thin line of pus trailed down the player's cheek.

The puck dropped, and Perera kicked it back to Arvidsson. The sound of skates carving through ice brought Brandon back into focus. Looking over his shoulder, he curled towards the opposing blue line. The one-eyed winger was covering Perera, leaving only one Saguenay defender on the right side. Perera kept taking whacks at people's shins, drawing them in to return the favour. Finding a little space, Arvidsson zipped a pass right through to Brandon. He took it on his backhand, and transitioned quickly over the blue line. The chaos stirred up by his scrappy centre had afforded him a one-on-one chance in the offensive zone. Just above the circle, a Nordique defender closing in fast. He had to make a move.

With a quick peek to his left, he saw that Bear had broken free from the scrum. He was streaking in against the boards, but the other defender was right with him. Brandon thought about faking a pass, but the odds of fooling anyone with that were low. The defender ahead of him had a pretty wide stance, leaving a lot of space between his legs. That was enough.

Pulling the puck wide, Brandon head-faked one way and took off in the other. He quickly tapped the puck through the defender's legs, and caught up with it on the other side. Alone against the goalie, he saw daylight in the top right corner. A second later, the puck was in the back of the net.

All nervous energy exploded outward as Brandon jumped into the air. He had just scored a goal. In the show. In his first game. Against Remy Baptiste! The crowd was so loud, and his teammates were so excited, he hardly noticed the cross-check to the ribs he took after scoring.

Sore and elated, he skated by the bench to bump fists with the rest of the team. Somewhere in the crowd, his folks were watching. Having a son who scored goals on

Hockey Night would definitely get them a little more respect around the neighbourhood. Maybe it would finally help them forget that time when mom put the People's flag out late on New Canada Day.

As he sat down on the bench, Coach Skinner gave Brandon a pat on the back. "Great goal, kid. Keep 'em coming. But keep your head up, there's still a lot of hockey to play."

...

Shovelling the slop after a game never really got any easier. Sure, a lot of it was held together by the snow kicked up by skates and sticks, but the sheer amount of viscera made for a slippery job. Most of it ended up in buckets, which would then be dumped into special dumpsters and left to melt for a while. The league didn't want anyone's usable organs going out with the rest of the garbage. It was too hard to pull the good stuff out of the fresh snow without damaging anything. Plus, some of the older guys still had gold teeth, or better yet—pacemakers. Valuable bits these days.

Marcus was on his hands and knees, trying to see if any of these unlucky players were brave or stupid enough to head out on the ice wearing any personal effects. Sometimes a chain would show up, maybe a bracelet. No precious metals, of course. But still, every once in a while something shiny could be snuck out of the arena and gifted to the wife. Today, no such luck.

Somebody had been eating boxed mac and cheese, that was for sure. The little elbow noodles spread out across the concrete flooring, partially digested. They sure weren't neon orange any more. Marcus wondered if the poor guy knew that would be his last meal. If he had, would he have tried to scrounge up something a little fancier?

The wheels of two garbage cans roared against the ground as another member of the ice crew pushed them toward the garage door. On the other side of that metal maw awaited the currently unlocked dumpsters. A couple more trips and they would be full. After that, the managers would come around and seal them up for the night. He nodded at the can-toting man, and returned to the sloshing human slime. The smell used to bother him, but now it was just part of the job. There was another crew member wading around across the room, wearing a face mask with a clothespin over her nose. She wasn't quite used to the stench.

A high-pitched beeping alerted everyone around to the Zamboni's imminent arrival. The crew cleared the way, allowing the machine to back up towards the garage door. The thing was filled with enough human remains, no need to let it crush someone else. Its tires sent ripples through the blood, bile, and stomach acid, which lapped up against Marcus' boots. As he looked down, his red-tinted reflection was rendered unrecognizable by the wake. He stepped back again, and felt the crunch of what could only be lost teeth beneath his sole.

The machine's arrival signalled the approaching end of their shift, so everyone grabbed their push brooms and got to sweeping. Liquid on the floor rushed towards the garage door behind the Zamboni, resulting in a torrent rushing into the open air. As they finished clearing out most of the goop, the resurfacer's tank lifted into the air. The hatch opened, and out came over a hundred cubic feet of collected snow, flesh, and bone. Immediately Marcus noticed a thumb sticking right out. A couple of teeth shone white against the red backdrop, and an eyeball looked right at him. Together, these loose parts built the visage of a smiling athlete, wordlessly communicating that he was a-ok.

As the machine pulled away from the snow bank, the tank lowering back onto its frame, some snow at the bottom shifted. Everyone else was putting their brooms away and heading to their lockers, but Marcus stuck around. He saw something uncovered by the shifting snow; a piece of jersey sticking out. Approaching cautiously, he kicked some red slush away, splattering the surrounding ground. The jersey was almost entirely dyed red, so he couldn't be sure what team it belonged to. Home was wearing their blues tonight, and the visitors had their away jerseys on—all white.

Attempting to pull the jersey out of the snow, Marcus found it wouldn't budge. It was still attached to something. A quick wash and it would be good as new, right? He could trade this to some hardcore fan for rations, or maybe a few cans of beer. He yanked harder, and felt a little give. A wet, sucking noise filled the air as it popped free.

The snow above avalanched down into the open space. The jersey wasn't stuck under something, or attached to anything, it was still being worn. Somehow, an entire headless torso had made it into the tank. Chopped off right at the base of the neck. Both arms were still attached, now mangled into mincemeat. Marcus flipped the body over to check the crest on the front. Thrashers. He didn't recognize the number on the back, though. 56… Must've been a rookie. He wasn't too worried about star power; jerseys were always worth something. Maybe someone would have fond memories of the kill on the ice.

It took a little wrestling to pull free, especially with the poor kid's arms the way they were, but Marcus walked home from the arena with his treasure discreetly tucked under his jacket. He shook his head.

"Buddy probably wasn't keeping his head up."

THE COLONOSCOPY

KAY HANIFEN

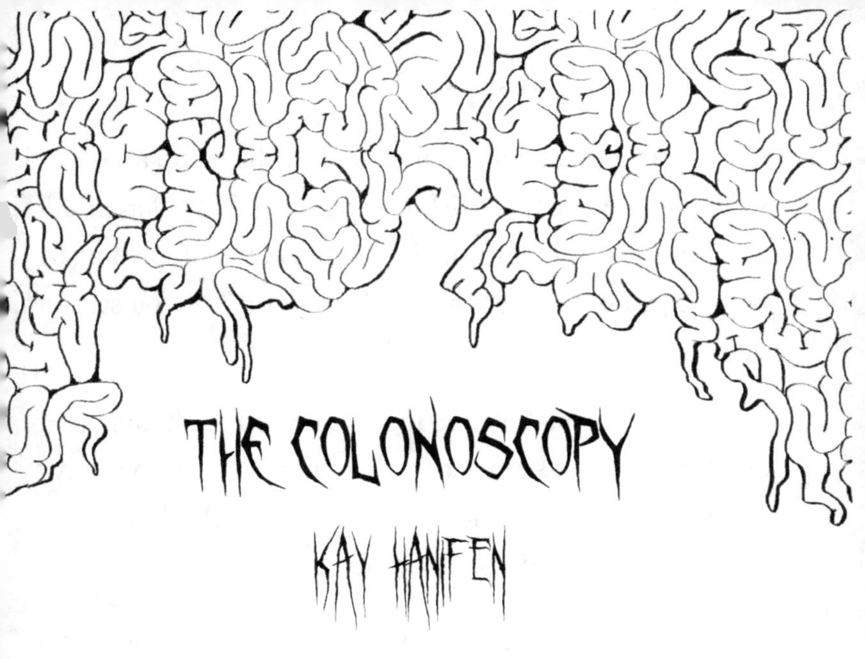

It had been three weeks since Christine last defecated. She knew she should *probably* see a doctor, but aside from the fact that she hadn't made that particular sacrifice to the porcelain throne in the past few weeks, she felt fine. No pain, no bloating, no feeling that something was stuck in her rectum. She simply hadn't felt the urge to go, not since her trip to the middle of the Amazon Rainforest. She'd heard of Montezuma's Revenge, but not extreme constipation like this.

Regardless, she was going to get a colonoscopy in two days, so she would be cleared out soon enough anyway.

"Green and blue jello are both stirred up and setting in the fridge," her PhD student and assistant, Laura, told her the day before she had to begin the prep. "I also bought you some beef and chicken broth. Are you sure you don't want me to hang around tomorrow?"

"And what? Watch me shit myself for hours on end?" Christine asked, staring into the fridge at the truly daunting amount of gelatin and Gatorade. She'll never look at the stuff the same way again.

"I could hang out. We could do a movie marathon or binge trashy reality TV to keep your mind off things." Laura seemed to have developed a crush on Christine during their journey through the wilds of the Amazon together. Nothing bonds two people quite like surviving together in a jungle while studying water-borne parasites.

"You're already driving me there and back, *and* helping me with my liquid diet. You've done more than enough, and I'm very grateful—but I think I'd prefer to be left on my own tomorrow." That way, Laura would only be around for the aftermath of the upcoming bowel explosion. Talk about a major turn-off. Christine rarely had crushes, so she didn't want to ruin this one with a brown out. "I promise I'll take my medicine and obey all the instructions."

"If you're sure. I could just be there for support."

Christine laughed. "I don't need an emotional support shit buddy. But thank you. Really."

Laura threw her arms around Christine and gave her a squeeze. "Call me if you need me."

"I will."

That night, Christine ate like a woman on death row—pizza, pasta, and a single slice of grocery store tres leches cake for dessert. The instructions never said when she needed to stop eating solid food, so she settled on midnight. That would give her more than twenty-four hours to purge that shit from her system. Given how constipated she was, that should hopefully be enough time.

This was her first colonoscopy, after all, so she wasn't entirely sure what to expect.

Christine woke the next morning and didn't bother changing out of her pajamas like she normally did. After all, she had preparations to make. 8.3 ounces of laxatives were to be dissolved into 64 ounces of lemon-lime Gatorade. When it was time to clear out, the doctors recommended drinking the mixture with ice and a straw to make it go down easier, so she made sure to have it on hand. Then, she napped to stave off hunger. After all, she probably wasn't getting any sleep that night.

When she woke that afternoon, Christine ate an obscene amount of lime and blue raspberry Jello, her stomach feeling sick and sloshy by the second bowl. It was the closest thing to full she knew she would feel for the next twenty-four hours.

Early in the afternoon, she took the two Bisacodyl tablets to help prevent gas. Then, at five o'clock, had her first cup of laxatives. One Eight-ounce cup every twenty minutes for the next hour. By the end, she would have consumed half the solution and would drink the rest five hours before her procedure. It was all a literal pain in the ass, but otherwise straightforward.

Her stomach began to rumble halfway through the second glass. With a sigh, Christine sucked up the last bit, paused the creature feature she was watching, and made her way to the bathroom.

Sitting on the toilet, Christine waited. And waited. And waited. Eventually, a gust of wind blew through her cheeks, but by then, it was time for another dose. She got up, grabbed another cup, and began to drink the yellow-gold sluice. Was it supposed to take this long to work?

Her stomach rumbled again. No, not rumbled. It *writhed* like a snake under her skin. Christine gasped and dropped her emptied drink in shock, ice and residual liquid spilling out onto the floor. Something was making her way through her bowels, and she could feel every single movement.

Ignoring the mess on the floor, she ran back to the bathroom as the wriggling made its way to her lower guts. Taking a seat on the toilet, she pushed, bearing down to rid herself of it.

A foul-smelling liquid poured from her anus, the odor of bile and rot. And then—something solid came wriggling, stuck halfway out, clinging to her as she tried to push it the rest of the way into the toilet.

A parasite. She had a parasite. Was that the root of her constipation?

Pushing was not working, so Christine stood up, reached back, pinched the end of the parasite and pulled. And kept pulling. The worm had to be at least a foot long.

She gasped as it came free, whipping back and forth like a furious snake. "What the fuck?" she shrieked, throwing it into the toilet and slamming the lid down. It rattled the top, so, in a panic, she sat on it, covering her mouth in horror.

Only for that horror to be doubled when she realized which hand she'd used to cover her mouth. Retching, she vomited foamy, clear liquid into the sink, and then, upon looking in the mirror and seeing the oily black smear on her face, she retched again. Once she got her nausea under control, she cleaned off the foul mark and thoroughly washed her hands.

Then her stomach writhed again. There were *more* of them?

Black liquid flowed down her legs as she staggered upstairs to her full bathroom, rather than the half-bath she'd been using on the main floor. Stripping down, Christine turned on the shower and sobbed as the second parasite made its way out of her bowels. This one was just as stubborn as the first, forcing her to pull it the rest of the way out. But *unlike* the first, she had enough time to examine this one.

The worm was black with iridescent ridges. Its shimmering cilia shook like leaves in a stiff breeze, feeling around and finding nothing but air while the suckers puckered as it struggled against her with surprising strength. It was mesmerizing—even as it splattered the remains of her excrement all over the bathroom.

But she already had the toilet parasite as a sample. She didn't need another live one.

Grabbing her shampoo bottle, she raised it above her head, ready to deliver the killing blow.

Wait!

Christine stopped mid-swing, her arm still in the air. Frozen in place. She wasn't sure if it was really her or the command of something else within preventing her from delivering the killing blow.

Because that… *thing* spoke to her.

Clear as day, the parasite living in her guts told her to wait. It was *intelligent*. It *communicated* with her. Scientific fascination warred with her horror and disgust.

Christine's been studying parasites her whole life, living with the stigma the creatures she studied brought, and not caring about what others thought in the slightest.

Because here's the thing about parasites: they're not inherently bad. Nothing in nature truly is evil. It simply is. Like all living beings, the number one mandate of a parasite is to survive long enough to produce offspring. She didn't want to play host to *sentient worms*, but if they were truly able to communicate with her, she should probably hear them out.

She dropped the bottle of shampoo behind her, and in response, the frantic wriggling of the parasite seeming to slow underneath her hand. "What the fuck are you?"

Images flashed in her mind's eye, moving far too quickly for her to fully comprehend.

Darkness punctuated by lights. Fire. Heat. The feeling of falling. Cool water. A mouth. Some place dark and warm. Safety. Hunger. Satiation. Growth. Reproduction.

Adoration. So much love for its host and the nursery tubes that feed and protect. Singing a song of devotion while cradled in that warm darkness. The feeling of being loved in return.

But then space growing too small to fit the bodies, the warm nursery tubes becoming prisons. The sound of ripping flesh and the feeling of hunger fully sated. Grief. Then, floating again in cool waters. Waiting for another mouth to take them in.

Now, awakening. Fear. The host expelling them too soon. Killing them. So much pain and terror.

Christine came back to herself with a gasp. No longer caring about the bile and excrement covering her hands, she brought one to her face and wiped away the tears.

She felt it. She felt the love they had for her, the same way a mother might feel the love of her unborn child.

Though a part of her was nauseated by the images of worms eating and growing inside her until her intestines burst open from the strain—Christine also knew that she couldn't let them die. If she was interpreting the images correctly, these parasites were proof of sentient alien life. This was a discovery that would change the course of history and human understanding of intelligence beyond the bounds of this planet.

But you also can't be the only host.

The thought took her aback. She didn't want to infect others. The ethics of that idea alone were a nightmare.

But that's a lie. You do. You want to understand.

Her guts spasmed, the laxatives hard at work forcing the contents of her bowels from her body. This wouldn't do.

Water samples. She had brought home some water samples from the Amazon to study. But she wasn't sure if, at this stage of development, the worms would be able to live in them.

"If I put you in water samples from your native habitat, will you survive?" she asked the one in her hands.

An intense hunger overcame Christine, making her double over. And suddenly, she couldn't breathe. She was exposed and starving and burning in the bright sun.

Food. Where is food? Where is safety? Mother? Mother, We are afraid.

The message was clear. She knew what she had to do. The thought nauseated her, but they wouldn't be able to survive without their host. Suppressing a gag, Christine opened her mouth and lifted the parasite by the tail. It wriggled eagerly as she lowered it down her throat, trying her best not to taste it as she swallowed.

Once, she had been so sick with the flu that she emptied her stomach and kept vomiting until nothing but a dark green bile flowed from her lips. The worm tasted of that bile and like the moldy peach she once ate on a dare. Though her guts rebelled, heaving and threatening to expel the worm, she managed to swallow without vomiting. It landed in her stomach and then writhed, shifting around in her antrum before worming into her small intestine through the pyloric sphincter.

Once it settled, Christine let out a sigh of relief. But that was short-lived when she remembered the worm she had abandoned in the toilet downstairs.

Save it! Save it!

She staggered to her feet, hoping it wasn't too late. A waterborne organism adapted to the chemical composition of the Amazon likely would not survive for long in a toilet. It would be like putting a saltwater fish in tap water.

Her guts grumbled. Because of the laxatives or the agitated parasites living in her gut, Christine wasn't sure. It felt like her intestines were shifting around, making it harder for her to move faster than a vague stumble in the direction of the downstairs toilet.

More foul-smelling liquid trickled from her asshole, but she didn't care. All she cared about was the organism she had left to die.

Reaching the bathroom, she threw open the toilet lid. The parasite moved sluggishly, but it was still alive. She picked it up and was about to shove it in her mouth when she heard a collective cry.

Stop!

Images assaulted her mind: *The weakened parasite dropping into her stomach. The agony of burning. Dissolving into nothing but waste.*

Apparently, the mouth was not feasible. Christine was running out of time. Soon, the worm would die in her hands.

But a mouth wasn't the only orifice she had.

Hiking her leg on the toilet seat, she bent over and brought the parasite's head right to her anus. And then, like administering a tampon into the wrong hole, she pushed it inside. Realizing what she was doing, it began to wriggle up her rectum, into her large intestine, through to her small intestine. She sighed with relief. *Safe*. It was now safe inside her.

But for how long?

They'd soon grow too big for her intestines to hold. She would die, *they* would die, and the scientific discovery of the century would be lost to the autopsy table or a jar of corpses in formaldehyde in a medical oddities museum. No one would know that she carried genuinely intelligent extraterrestrial life inside her.

Not unless you share the love.

Heading back upstairs and rinsing the worms oily by-product off her buttocks in the shower, Christine considered her options. One name seemed to fill her mind, creating an urge like no other.

Laura, Laura, Laura. Got to call Laura.

Christine changed into a fresh pair of pajamas and cleaned up the spilled laxative. No more of that would pass her lips tonight. Not when she knew when to call forth her children upon command.

Children. When had she started thinking of them as children? But their love for her felt just like the love an infant has for a mother; A love born of comfort, of knowing that she will provide them food, shelter, and safety.

Her phone was right where she left it on the coffee table, the screen lighting up with messages from Laura checking in. She was such a sweet girl, and deserved all the love in the world.

Picking up her phone, Christine dialed her number. Laura picked up on the second ring. "Hey, is everything okay? You didn't answer my texts. I just figured you were on the toilet, but I was starting to get worried," Laura said.

"I'm fine." Christine bit her lip. "But do you remember what I said about not needing an emotional support shit buddy? I think I might have changed my mind."

"Okay, I'll be right over."

"Thank you, Laura."

When they hung up, Christine made up a pot of tea, poured one out for herself and another for her guest. Then, she crushed a sleeping pill in her friend's drink and stirred until it dissolved. Her stomach rumbled and stirred from the laxatives still in her system and partly from the worms moving inside her.

Sat at her kitchen table, she nursed her tea in one hand and idly chewed a fingernail on the other. And she waited.

Her friend knocked on the door a few minutes later. When Christine opened it, Laura gave her a hug. "Hey, how are you feeling?"

"Not great. You have no idea how *weird* this whole process has been."

"I know." Sighing, she stepped inside and shut the door behind her. "I am so glad that mine isn't for another fifteen years. But hey, it's better than dying of colon or rectal cancer, right?"

"Right." Christine led her to the kitchen. "I made you a cup of tea—just how you like it."

"Are you sure you don't need *me* to get you anything? How's your Gatorade supply?" Laura took a seat, but her gaze was intent on the fridge.

"I'm fine. I mostly just wanted company, if that's okay." Christine took her seat and sipped her drink, watching with satisfaction as Laura did the same. "I hope I'm not keeping you from anything important."

Laura shook her head. "I was just going to process some specimens tonight. You're a lot more fun to be around than river water."

They chatted idly and drank their tea. Soon, Laura started yawning. "Sorry. I guess I'm more tired than I thought. Jet lag and scientific bureaucracy really takes it out of you!"

Christine finished her own glass, hands shaking and abdomen twitching in anticipation. "Don't worry about it. Would you like to nap on my couch?"

"I mean, I came to spend time with you, not—" She yawned again. "Man, I don't know what's come over me. I—"

Christine caught Laura as she collapsed and laid her down, carefully opening her mouth and clearing her airways. Then, she pulled her pants down, felt the wriggling in her guts as one worked its way through her large intestine. The foul-smelling oil that preceded the children no longer bothered her. In fact, the odor had become almost… comforting.

She pulled the worm free and held it over Laura's open mouth. Instead of climbing eagerly inside like the one she swallowed, it twisted, curling up around her hand like a snake.

Her children are waking already. Not an adequate host.

Christine supposed she shouldn't be surprised that Laura was carrying them too. They drank from the same river, after all. Though currently separated from one another, the worms seemed to share a collective hive mind. They wanted to be reunited.

She wondered, idly, if this was the true root of Laura's seemingly inexplicable attraction to her, and Christine's own interest, despite never having romantically desired another person before. Still, love was love, and she basked in the glow of Laura's affection the same way that she did with the worms now that they had awoken.

Christine didn't bother pulling up her pants, Winnie-the-Poohing it as she carried Laura to the couch. When the time came, she wouldn't be the only one waking up.

Then she showered again and waited. If her friend was not a suitable new home, she needed to find someone else. And she had the perfect candidates in mind.

Laura woke an hour later, a dazed smile on her face. "Christine? What are you doing here?"

"It's my house," Christine replied, smiling warmly back at her. She could feel it. She could feel Laura and her worms' love, and the love of those inside her own intestines. It was like basking in spring sunshine.

She sat up and took Christine's hand. "I had the most wonderful dream. Though, it wasn't a dream, was it? They're still inside me, and they're in you too, aren't they?"

"They are." Christine closed her eyes, feeling the warmth in her chest as the twelve worms inside her expressed their affection.

Without thinking about it, they leaned in close, their mouths connecting in a kiss, and it was like the whole world sang with their perfect unity. They could be in that embrace forever. But there was one matter to worry about first. They needed more hosts.

#

Dr. Carroway washed his hands as he prepared for the procedure. He had three colonoscopies scheduled for today, which was a bit of a caseload, but not too bad, all things considered. His first patient, a forty-five year old female, was already in the surgical bed, her leg hiked up and anus presenting for the probe.

Before administering the sedative, he shook her hand. "Don't worry. You'll just take a nap, and as soon as you wake up, you can eat again."

She grinned in a way that should have been self-deprecating, but there was a sort of dreaminess to her smile. "Good. You have no idea how hungry I am."

His anesthesiologist administered the drugs and her eyelids fluttered shut. Soon, she's fast asleep.

"I am now inserting the probe," Dr. Carroway announced as he began the procedure. He threaded the camera through her rectum, taking care not to tear or puncture any skin. A perforated bowel was rare, but not impossible, so he needed to be careful.

The trouble began in the large intestine. The camera picked up a long, black object. At first, he thought that she had not fully cleared the excrement from her bowels. But then, it moved. *A tapeworm?*

Most worms, though, were white. Why have pigmentation when you will never see the light of day? But this one was black like a garter snake.

"The hell is that?" one of the nurses asked. Her brows were furrowed with confusion and curiosity.

He shook his head. "I have no idea. The laxatives should have cleared everything out, parasites included. I've never seen anything like this before."

And then the worm latched onto the camera, wrapping itself around it. He used every single ounce of willpower to slowly remove the camera instead of ripping it out of this woman's body like his instincts told him to.

It didn't take long to remove the probe… and the thing attached to it. He lifted it up to get a better look in the light. "What are you—*urk*!"

None of this should be possible. A tapeworm could not purposefully wrap itself around a colonoscopy camera, moving with the strength of a snake. And it *definitely* shouldn't be able to leap from the camera to his open mouth and force its way down his throat like salmon swimming upstream during spawning season.

He gagged on the taste of bile and shit, but the worm was stubborn. It forced itself down his throat, no matter how hard he tried to pull it out. It hit his stomach, made its way through the pyloric sphincter, and into his small intestine.

He felt it. All of it. But more than anything, he felt the worm's love as it wallowed in his food waste. He'd always been married to the job, never having time to settle down and have kids. This adoration must be what fathers feel holding their child for the first time.

"Are you okay?" the anesthesiologist asked, giving his shoulder a concerned squeeze.

Dr. Carroway felt the grin spread across his face as a strange euphoria enveloped him. "I feel wonderful." His legs seemed to move of their own accord as he shut and locked the door. He met their terrified gazes before glancing down at the other worms crawling their way out of his patient's anus.

The anesthesiologist and two nurses made a beeline for the door, but he blocked their exit.

"Daniel, what the fuck?"

Dr. Carroway just smiled. "Christine, Laura, and I can't be the only hosts. A love like this must be shared with everyone."

One of the nurses shrieked as a worm climbed up her leg. She tried to shake it off, it held fast, working its way inside her through the most convenient orifice—her anus. And then there were two.

He grabbed a worm while the now infected nurse restrained the other. Forcing her mouth open, he dropped it down her throat. As she choked, sputtered, and gagged, he felt when the worm settled into place. Another soul added to the collective. She was one of them now. And she would help her fellow nurse restrain the anesthesiologist while Carroway administered the last of the worms.

All the while, Christine slept peacefully, a smile playing across her lips as the worms gifted her the sweet dream: herself and Laura wandering among the stars.

"**W**hat's good PopStars! it's ya girl Poppy, and I am SO FREAKING excited to be here today!"

Here squeezing every last drop of cash and attention out of you fucking losers. Three thousand of you watching, two hundred bucks in tips already and I haven't even done anything yet. P.T. Barnum was talking about you, chat.

"Today I am at El Gordo Guapo Cantina,"

More like El Gringo Crappo.

"Trying their newest challenge,"

Newest desperate spange for relevance.

"The Case o' Quesabirria challenge!"

Whose failson came up with that name? These things aren't even in a case, it's just a wall of greasy cheese flaps and a trough of sour meat sauce. Hurl.

"That's right, it's a birria challenge! Beer-ya? Buh-REE-ah? Berry-ya? Like, *tongue click* uhmuhgaw I don't even, like, know how you say it, but you know what I mean!"

I mean *that I hate you people for thinking this 'skinny ditz who can pack away food' bit is cute, desirable, or even fucking believable. But I can't quit you.*

"Mmkuh, for those of you who don't kno-ow, birria is thee newest trend, and it is SO good. It's a spicy beef broth with meat in it… I mean I think it's beef—or maybe it's cow?"

Acting like an idiot is great bait for rage comments. All engagement is good engagement, bay-bee. See, look, just like clockwork. One wave of 'beef IS cow, dumbass,' 'she can't be serious,' and 'OK, Some children left behind,' followed by a salvo of defense from my pathetic simps, and a tennis match of arguments about whether I'm faking being dumb. Every returned volley moves me further up the Top of the Now charts and nets me more viewers, more money, more attention.

"But ya! As you can see, it is all right here in front of me, and it is *massive*! We have got not one, not two but *thirty* classic cheese quesadillas…"

I say it like kwessadillyas. Some dipshit tips me $50 'For Spanish lessons, crying emoji.' Thanks, dipshit, you fuckin' dipshit, dipshit. God, I'm so much better than these fucks, it makes me mad sometimes that I even let them pay to address me.

"Thirty quesadillas, just like, normal ones, BUT, look at this absolute bucket of birria sauce, it's a half GALLON—ohmygaw of this delicious spicy, savory, *spicy* sauce, and I need to eat it all in… how long is it again?"

I remember full well that I have a half hour. It's good to ask the help, though, makes it look like I care about the plebs and gives dawdlers more time to tune in.

"Umm, let me check," says the waitress, Maghkeighleigh.

It's a half hour.

"Olaf!" she yells, "How long for the challenge?"

It's a half hour.

"Olaf!"

Olaf pls

"YA WHATCHER?"

Olaf!

"How long for the challenge?"

It's still thirty minutes.

"I need to check the website."

"Well, *I* could check the website, don't you just know?"

"Then you go check the website!"

"Okay, fine, I'll check the website!"

"Don't bother, I'm already gonna check!"

"Well so'm I!"

"Well so'm *I* so'm I!"

So'm I gonna gauge my goddamn eyes out on stream, that'll get some views.

"Thirty minutes!" they shout in unison, having checked the Jesus fucking shit website. I can hear the Hat Dance playing asynchronously through shitty speakers on their respective devices.

"Okay, thirty minutes, THEENKS Maghkeighliegh!"

A little heavy on the cheer, there, Pops. Reel it in. Five thousand tuned in, and another two hundred bucks, just for being moi. *I suppose I could give them what they want.*

"So if I finish all of this in thirty minutes, which, I dunno… it's like, so much food!"

They fucked up choosing thirty minutes. That is trivially easy. A hungry normie or committed stoner could do this.

"Then I get the whole meal free, instead of—how much if I lose?"

I'm not letting this turn into Who's On First with the goof troop again.

"Oh, $75, I remember! And I get a sweet, sweet T-shirt, and my picture on their wall of fame. Now so far only one person has beaten this challenge so far, the one and only king of competitive eating, Buford Glutz, everybody give it up!"

Give it up before his fuckin' heart does. He's my only real competition as long as he lives, but he's not making that look like a long time. He can't keep it up. Yeah, he's got twice as many viewers than me, but he's been around five years longer. And we go bite for bite even though he's three times my size. He's not special. Not like me.

"Okay, what do you think, PopStars, are we going to get this done?"

My in-person crowd goes wild. I used to hire people to come to my challenges, but when I got famous, it would become a liability if I got exposed, sooooo I paid them to shut up and fuck off. People started showing up organically anyway. Now I spend that money on security.

"Okay, can I get a countdown and then let's *start that timer*! If you're not subscribed, please smash that like," smash my brains out with a hammer, "hit that bell," hit some sense into me. For this, I go to Juilliard? "And of course, if you aren't subscribed yet, what are you *doing*?"

What you're doing is not rewarding a performance artist whose work was too provocative, so now she makes a living doing some Frankenstein mash up of lolcowing, fetish content, schadenfreude, and town square pillory tomato-dumpster. But I've grown this channel from nothing to huge in just a year. I'm so close to a million followers, a golden stream trophy, and proper sponsorship, I can practically smell it over the greasy feast in front of me. Oh shit, right, sponsorship. God, this is depressing enough to make me wanna commit sewer slide.

"But first, this video is sponsored by Therapr, where you can talk to a licensed therapist who will definitely help and is being paid adequately and won't sell your data, all for just ten dollars for your first session if you use the promo code P-O-P-P-Y-E-A-T-S. Fam, it's hard out there, on god, no cap fr fr. Depression is sadge, therapy is poggers, and there's nothing L about getting help. Your mental health is GOATED. Take care of it."

Now back to me, eating thirty diarrhillas.

"Okay, let's get this started in three! Two!" I pick up my first quesadilla. It almost slips out of my hands, it's so lardy. 'One' and 'go!' happen around me, and I turn off my brain and get into the zone.

The big secret of competitive eating is not to eat. I know—that sounds like contrarian bullshit, or Star Wars level Buddhism, but it's true. You have to stop thinking about it like it's the same eating you do for pleasure or nutrition. It's just the mechanical act of using your hands to make the stuff bite sized, bringing it to your face, then moving your jaw like a marathoner's legs, never stopping the machine until it's done. Not like real sports, where your muscles give out eventually. It's just about wanting it bad enough. And I want it.

There are little techniques here and there, sure; When to use water or sauce, what to eat in what order for temperature, leaving spicy stuff for the end. For example, here, a noob would dip the quesadillas in the broth as she goes, because that's how you eat this normally. But the broth is visibly steaming around its clots and embolisms— it's way too hot right now. The cheese has the opposite problem. Once it cools and hardens into a glue-gun stick, it's murder on your jaw, so those are going first. This is all nitpicking though, really, we're talking a 5-percent difference. The real job is just to lowkey dissociate, forcing your body through the motions. And who hasn't been there, amirite ladies?

Either you win, or it was designed to be impossible, which does happen. They've tuned it too easy here, but they overclocked it in other joints; sometimes because they don't know what they're doing, sometimes because they just want you to lose. Anyway, I digest, hehe.

"Oh wow. This is SO good you guys, you should *definitely* come here and eat, like a normal amount of food ey-luh-mao!" *It's a lie to say it's good, but only because I have no idea how it tastes, smells, or feels. The part of me that could tell these things is simply not at home right now. I don't want to give away my strat entirely on cam, so I go for a costly but tactical dunk. A part of me yells that it's still too hot and that it's burning our mouth raw, but I take that part of me out back and Ol' Yeller that weakass bitch. I'm here to win.*

I adjust my tank top so that the inevitable (intentional) spilled sauce lands on my cleavage. That always gets clipped and shared on both PG and X-rated sites. Same clip, very different purposes, same outcome: more engagement, more sympathy, clout, followers, fans, and money. The money is the least of it, really. I need the high score. I need the validation, the prizes, the awards; I want to be known. I want to be talked about. I want to be *famous*. That's all.

When I put away the last quesadilla, the fucking waitress has turned the restaurant TV on. What is she thinking?

"Oh ehm, issCUSE mee? Could we turn it off pleeeeez just for the cameras?"

I hear a few words from the TV newscaster over annoying alarmed chatter from the plebs. 'Transmitted in edible meat, especially beef—highly contagious—similar to Ebola—quarantine—national guard—immediately.'

Then chaos. Air raid sirens hit, and people stampede—some fuck knocks over my tripod. *They're ruining the video!* People are going to think I cheated! What the fuck, don't they know who I am, what I'm doing here? Don't they know they're getting in *my* way?

"Still eatingggg!" I grab the bucket of sauce and start chugging desperately. I need to *win.* I down the half gallon of stew and stick my tongue out, showing everyone there that I did it, I won!
Nobody is even watching me.

One of my security picks me up abruptly under the armpits and carries me out. It's too fast, and spicy sour redness shoots out of my mouth like a garden hose. "I'm *hooooosh* I'm the best! *Wooouuuughhh ptuh!* How are my likes? Get my—*hurrr*—phone! I can't see my likes!" I puke on some dumb baby in a high chair. "I can't see my—" *splash-waaaah!* "Likes!"

****

The cow plague killed every bovine on Earth, and a tenth of the world's human population during its first year. Well guess *what,* bitches, pressure makes diamonds and I. Am. Thuh-*riving!* I was *shooketh* at first, sure that mass restaurant closure would mean no more challenges, which means no more content. Nope!

Turns out, hungry people want to watch people eat. They eat their little instant ramen—no red packets, of course—watch *me* eat like a queen, and pretend they're on my level. Of course, some hate-watch me. I even got a video essay or two about how I was on some *Marie Antoinette shit,* but, like I said before, engagement is engagement.

Ever resourceful, I cut a deal with the diner under my apartment. I single-handedly kept them afloat during the initial lockdown and beef-burning that bankrupted so many others. I had the cash, they had the inventory, and I make back what I spend a hundred-fold in *every* video. Then I figured—why waste money buying *from* them? So I pretended to have money issues until they were on the verge of bankruptcy and fuckin' *bought* the place! Sorry Dimitrios, your family had a great run, but it's my place now. Turns out "family owned since 1964" just isn't as valuable as "ghost kitchen-slash-mukbanger's personal chef."

Like any artist, I suffer for my craft. Nobody wants to watch me eat a salad, or like, one pizza. Nobody watches normal people having normal sex, right? It has to be five figures of calories or nobody's watching. I experimented, of course; I bought a dozen of those square watermelons to see if "Cute Girl's $1500 MELONS?" would play, but it barely did better than the fifty egg omelet video or the one where I got in a kiddie pool full of mac n' cheese and ate my way out. Point being, I haven't had a solid shit since lockdown, and you could see your reflection in my skin from all the grease.

"Thank you so much for tuning in everyone, one hundred pepperoni pizza bagels was tough, but you know ya girl Pops was gonna crush it!"
Oof, I'm gonna Totino's Party Puke.

"K likeansubscribeandsmashthatbell BYE!" I slam my sodium-trembling hand on the keyboard and make a run for the bathroom before I hork up a kid's birthday party. I wash up, get back to my stream setup and look at myself in the mirror-but-better of my webcam. The fuck is that in the corner of my nose? Christ, that zit is sinister. It's the size of a pea, and looks like a fucked up titty. Swollen, creamy with a red bullseye and protruding peppercorn in the middle. I move closer to my webcam, looking at my image on the monitor. I put my finger next to the pimple and pull down on the skin to get a better look. My fingernail snags the zit's swollen poppy seed tip, and with a sound like snapping celery, the zit ejaculates all over the webcam.

The chat goes *wild*. Wait, what? The *chat?! FUCK!* I didn't close the stream in my haste to throw up! So they saw both that and this? Panicked, I unplug my PC, turn all the lights off, and get under the covers.

I'm ruined. It's all over. My blood pressure is too high for this stress. As I black out, I hope a stroke just fuckin' takes me out.

****

I wake up from a nightmare where I had to do a mukbang eating live kittens. My reality is worse: people might not love me anymore. The frozen bottle of vodka hurts my hands, but the hooch numbs me enough to look at my socials.

Yeah. It's as bad as I thought.

A couple hundred BingBongs already are up, clips of me puking off-cam and pus-squirting onto-cam. They've added that squirt sound effect. There's been enough time for a dozen or so reactors to do their thing, truly the Lyme-disease ticks of streaming. What I'm doing is performance art, okay? I'm holding a lens up to the ugliest impulses in modern society, and then these reactor fucks just watch my videos, go "wow" or "eww" and get a quarter as many views as me? *Vultures*!

I take another pull from the bottle, hold a breath, and check my VOD. Before last night's stream, I was at exactly 998,654 subscribers. But who's counting? So, *so* close to that beautiful rollover from k to M, so close to the *gold*. Today? 684,286 subs. Paid subscriptions have been halved. Last night's stream is the fourth-most-downvoted video on the internet, right between "Gorilla vs Fart Prank (Gone Wrong!)" and Paul Logan.

My inbox is predictable: The usual misogyny, SA-threats, links I'll never click, $2500 donation from PEENA, rapey mobile game—wait, *$2500 donation?* I click it, sure my sagging eyes are missing where there's a scam or a spoofed email. It looks legit, so I check my bank account. It is.

"Hi, OMG thank you so much! What!? Do I know you?" I strip, get up to take a shower but see three dots in chat. I sit my nekkid ass right back down.

"The Pimple Extrusion Enthusiasts of North America caught wind of your stream last night. I hope I can respectfully convey that that was the best video we've ever seen. It was like a perfect Bigfoot shot for cryptozoologists; it was a UFO filmed from three angles. It was our *Zapruder* film. If you can make content like that consistently, you can name your fee."

"How many of you are there?" I ask. Guess I'll need income, but the views are how I measure success.

"Ha." is all I get back.

****

A week of stomach churning research into pimple popping videos has taught me two things: more people watch them than did my mukbangs; and none of these creators have a fucking clue how to be famous. I'm gonna be so. Fucking. *Big*. I invest in a variety of masquerade masks; Each covers or reveals a different part of my face, so I can always pop something without revealing my identity. Not yet.

I put in an order downstairs for homefries, battered deep-fried bacon, two sampler platters, a cherry pie, and the oldest, most-used oil they have sitting around. I eat this and yap my way through an apology video on the ruins of my channel. Mental health this, stepping back that, let you down the other. What the fuck ever.

When I'm done, I publish the stream as a permanent video called "I Hear You (Apology)" and even turn monetization off for clout. It stings, since it gets crazy views and comments immediately, but an artist does not live on poutine and eggrolls alone. I start a second channel with a new email address, not linked to my mukbang one. I call it "Big Zitty Goth GF" and send the link to PEENA. Instantly, he—and I'm *sure* it is a he—replies:

"We look forward." and tips $250. I take the bucket of rusty fryer grease into the bathroom with me and get to work on my showstopper.

****

It only takes a month for me to become huge. I was worried the ellipsis of whiteheads on my jawline wouldn't be exciting enough for a first video, but some good lighting, a made-up story about my day, and a perfect triple pop blows their mind. I get magnifying mirrors, multiple cameras, and soon enough a two-minute video nets me the views I used to get for food challenges that took me out all day, and that's not even counting the toilet time after. Of course, I *do* start to eat even worse just to keep the zits flowing.

I read every article from doctors to beauticians to teen magazines about how to beat that *tough acne*, and I do the exact opposite of what I find. I bathe like a bachelor: pits and holes only. I touch my face *constantly*, and discover that massaging the base of those really deep cysts irritates them into producing more sebum. I turn my walk-in closet into a reverse sauna: a closet with a stool, and wall-to-wall dehumidifiers. I punch a hole in the wall to let the diner's grease vent pour into the room. With my kiddie pool under me to catch runoff, I ladle shortening over my head with the reverence of a flagellant. And every night, without fail, I take that bucket of old fryer grease, and I work on my showstopper. I go through a bucket a week now. I've started paying them to just fry literal food waste, all to make me more triple-burned oil. For my grand finale. For my close-up.

****

I harvest cottage cheese from my golf ball earlobe. Twenty thousand followers, five grand from PEENA. I get a really sore deep one on my shoulder, and set up cameras all around my yoga setup. I get down on my back and use a massage roller to push the wad of curdled vodka sauce around the zit, teasing, always teasing, until, BAM! A jubilee of sepsis. Fifty thousand, ten gees.

To celebrate a half million followers, I reveal that I was Poppy Eats the whole time. There had been some speculation, but the reveal video takes me halfway to a million in a *day*. To celebrate five million followers, I do a duet with CaulipowerNoze, a genuinely pathetic creature who started making popping content inspired by *me*. Now he's just about as famous because the poor fuck has the worst case of lifelong full body acne I've ever seen, all rosy craters and broken capillaries. His sob story has made him a star, even, *shudder*—my peer. I can't compete with that.

Good for him for making a buck out of tragedy. Some of us need to actually try.

When he's coming over, I hide away the buckets of fryer grease. He must never learn about my showstopper. I put a black tarp down and set up the shoot. And shoot we do. We're like old friends gossiping as we take turns mining for curds on each other's backs, legs, and folds. I do both his shoulders at once with my feet. The white vermicelli strands that explode out of him are so solid they stand right up, making him look like a fetid porcupine. When he touches my back to get at a really stubborn marble of a zit right above my ass, his hands are soft, and he's disarmingly gentle. Our stream takes him over one million, and me close to five, all in a day. Beauty and the Beast is a thing for a reason.

His departure is an awkward morning-after getaway. He stammers something about his sad existence; but I cut him off before he can get to the part where he says this was the best day of his life, or asks me out, or threatens to kill himself. Those are usually what happens at the end of these dribblings. I tell him I have stuff to do. No stranger to being disposable, he leaves, cringing. I've just peeled my bloody tank top off when I hear his phone ring, playing some anime theme song, on my kitchen counter. I put it all together the same instant as he bursts back into the apartment door he was too timid to close properly.

"Sorry, I—Oh! Oh, God! Poppy… You're--"

He's looking at my tits like he's a cartoon wolf about to fly through the air on the smell of a pie. "Your boob—I mean…" He closes the door behind him. "Sorry, but… wow. You've got thre—"

"It's okay," I coo, approaching. "It's fine."

The first slash glances off his tough, scarred neck wattle, but a harder stab does the trick. Those German kitchen knives don't fuck around. Two hundred pounds of cystic, apologizing meat hit the floor. I won't get the burgers from downstairs for a while.

****

Two months later and I'm out of fucking zits, and PEENA is losing patience. So are my fans. I've been religiously disgusting, only changing my sheets because whatever is going on with my body is leading to some pretty exciting sharts. I've been eating garbage, using the fry sauna, and drinking simple syrup like a fucking hummingbird at a feeder. And I look—well, I look real bad. But so did David Blaine when he came out of that ice cube. So do ultramarathoners shitting themselves across the finish line. So did Jesus out of the tomb. What true artist isn't changed by their process?

But I've popped zits everywhere I am allowed to show, and a few 'next-tos' that got me wrist-slaps or fines. People really hated the video of me popping the cherry tomato between my toes. I guess foot people and zit people have beef. I actually lost mad followers for that.

I'm doing my best to stall, doing vlogs, life updates... I even start playing video games and singing karaoke on stream. Nothing.

I lose one-percent of my subs every day. By the time I look like poor old Caulipower, I'm a nobody again. I can't bust out my showstopper yet, I need another hit to buoy me, so my close-up is seen by as many as possible.

I sigh and a zit on my scalp breaks in sympathy. Those *useless* fucking scalp zits, hiding among my hair where nobody can—oh!

I make an announcement for my biggest show yet, a week from today. I need to prep. Bleach my scalp so raw it crusts and flakes like a square pizza, then settles into sedimentary layers of grease, blood, skin, and scab. Sure enough, four days later, two-inch tall volcanoes sprout all over my scalp. Scissors take most of my hair off, leaving a layer of fuzz that'd be punk chic if I didn't look like a rotten apple.

The night of the stream, two million tune in. Not bad. The chat is full of warnings that this is my last chance. I've gotten good at putting makeup on my scarred skin, and I'm in a tux, giving off lesbian fuckboy energy that I don't hate. After a baroque introduction, it's time. I pause. Breathe in the moment before my return to fame. Breathe out. Turn to the side.

The clippers are on zero when I run them from behind my ear, up an unnatural straight line to my crown.

They shred hair and skin and pimple alike. The surface of my scalp is a primordial eruption as they catch, tear, jam, clear and continue. As if conducting Wagner, I run them a short cut here, a slash there, keeping a wet tempo. When I'm smooth and pouring, I come down from my reverie and look at my follower count.

What? It's plummeting! This was too gross, I guess. I jumped the shark. Turned the corner. Went too far. No. No, no, no. They're leaving me. My fans and devotees are leaving me!

The showstopper! I have to give them the showstopper. I rip my jacket off, then tear my shirt down the middle, my gray sports bra damp with pus lactation. That slows the mass exodus, alright. More even come back! Yes! *Yes*! I'm over four million! Here we go!

I pull the bottom of my bra up, lifting my bust up to my collarbone, then I give them the most memorable titty drop of their lives. My left breast bounces down. Then my right. Then my middle.

In between my acne-ravaged dugs is a new third: a soccer ball sized zit swirling like a porthole into a lava lamp ocean of blood, pus, and kombucha-floater scabs. It is an eye turned back on you miserable people, and it sees your cowardice. *This* is what you wanted, but only a fraction of you can admit to i—and now you're pussying out. I grip each of my outer tits from the outside, push them together around my precious baby, close my eyes, and *squeeze*.

The sound is a like hundred fireworks, the sensation a thousand throat-choked orgasms. The smell is a war crime. Then I open my eyes to the carnage.

I don't mean the mess, which is, of course, wall to wall. A pink poached egg dangles from my mic, but I don't mean that, either. I mean my subscriber count. It's plummeting as I watch it. Four million ticks down into the threes, then 3.8. 3.7… Fuck. The chat is flooded with cruel abandonment.

"Too far."

"Get help."

"Reported. Enjoy your permaban."

"This isn't fun anymore."

"She actually did it. She actually ruined boobs."

Then, I read a bolded message from PEENA.

"You are no longer of value to us. Goodbye."

No. No, no no nonono.

"Wait, chat, hole up fam, I… I've got more to pop, I can go back to normal content! Just hang on! Hey!" I scan my weeping body for anything, *anything* left to squeeze a little pus and validation out of. There's nothing. Head to toe, I'm spent. I've blown every load, pulled out every desperate stop I have, and I have no way to make them stay. My whole world is crumbling, right in front of my fucking eyes. In front of my… my…

Oh.

I go to the kitchen, get that German knife, put my face right in front of my webcam, and pull my eyelids open with my left hand. I dissociate like I used to while eating competitively. A weird alert sound from my computer almost takes me out of my meditative state, but I'm too good to be distracted *that* easy. Momma, I'm going off the high dive! Are you watching?

The big secret to enduring self-mutilation is not to feel the pain. I know, that sounds like contrarian bullshit, or Star Wars level Buddhism, but it's true. You have to stop thinking about it like it's the same kind of pain you feel when you bark your shin or get a paper cut. It's just the mechanical act of using your hands to slit your eyeball open across the middle with a paring knife, slipping your thumb and pointer into the back of your socket and pulling forward like you're milking a cancerous pig. Simple! Then you put the knife point in front of the other pupil, like you're examining its extra sharp tippy tip-tip, and you push. You twist. You churn. It's not like real pain, where your body refuses to let you hurt yourself. It's just about wanting it bad enough. And I want it.

I don't hear any chat notifications. I don't need to, to know that everybody's talking about me. Everyone's going to see what I've done and talk about me *forever*. I've done it. I'm enough.

When my dissociation begins to thaw, the pinging sound the computer made earlier rushes back to me. That urgent little alert, right before I took the knife to my eyes. I recognize that sound now. It's the sound it makes when your live stream is taken down by the mods.

Nobody even saw me jump.

I can't see anything.

My likes.

I can't see all my likes.

Casey comes in through the jalousie window, through the broken slats she kicked in the summer before. She clambers in the way a spider would: legs first, then arms, then the rest of her, until she's across the room and into bed with me.

She twists my nipple through the top sheet. "Are you awake?"

I am now.

When I first met Casey, she told me not to fall in love with her or anything. People always end up loving the wrong people. They fell over themselves for her all the time.

"I'm like one of those bugs that eats what they fuck," she told me.

Then she asked if I had any lip gloss, and if I was going to fall in love.

"Don't," she said. "I'm serious."

I do whatever Casey wants.

Outside, a truck with no muffler revs its engine. Bitches yowl from the puppy mill across the reservoir. Inside, my broken tower fan stutters left, then pivots right. Casey presses her sweaty tits to my sweaty neck and her lips to my cauliflower ear.

"I need you," she pants. "It's inside me. Deep, deep down, and you've got to get it out."

#

I used to work the graveyard shift at Our Lady of Mercy, in the ER. When I tell people that, they always ask if I have stories. They want to hear about strangers hurting in special, terrible ways.

The anecdotes came in on bank holidays and full moons. Any time people were feeling free and adventurous, a little lonely, or just plain bored. Hypodermic needles snapped off in urethras, cigarette butts smoldering in trachs. The expected butt stuff: lost dildos, lodged light bulbs. Jawbreakers. Joysticks. G.I. Joes.

Some nights, removals were half the job. Reaching up inside of people. Pulling things back out.

When I transferred to surgery, I struck up a friendship with an older doctor.

"It's psychological," she told me. "Everybody's always just trying to fill a hole."

In her youth, she'd worked in one of those one-horse, one-hospital Protestant counties, the kind where you couldn't buy hard liquor or objectionable literature or anything to do with sex.

On her first case as an attending, the paramedics wheeled in a woman who smelled like barbecue. When the doctor told the story, she paused there for effect.

"I haven't eaten ribs since."

It was an era before the mail order strap-on. So this woman and her girlfriend had been experimenting with their curling iron instead. Right shape. Right size. Convenient handle. In and out, building friction, making heat.

Until, at some point, the iron turned on. God knows why they left it plugged in. By the time it got hot enough to realize, this woman's anal cavity was a raw third-degree burn. The EMTs brought the iron in with her. It was covered in a thin, curling, crisped film, like a grilled bratwurst with burst skin.

So, after eight years of school and five as a surgical resident, my doctor friend spent her first official day on the job with her nose in a speculum-spread asshole, excising unviable rectal tissue. Then she had to install a colostomy bag, since until the wounds healed, the patient was in danger of sepsis every time she took a shit.

You'd think that was the worst part.

It wasn't.

The worst part was that, when this woman was finally released, she waited in the lobby for her girlfriend to come get her. For hours and hours, she sat there in a wheelchair, feces rerouting into a bag on her hip, biding time for a woman who never came.

#

"What's inside of you?" I ask Casey.

It's not a light bulb, or a cigarette. She promises she's not hurt.

It's just a tampon, she says. She put it in at lunchtime, tied one off and forgot about it. Then her boyfriend came over and fucked it up into her, so deep she can't reach it anymore.

"He thinks it's fully grody. He's not gonna touch it." She grips my biceps so tight, her press-ons bite half moons into my skin. "But you will. I know you will."

#

When I think about Casey, I think about Harlequin shrimp. I think about how they flip starfish on their backs and snip off all their little starfish feet, then eat their limbs, right down to the core.

The starfish is a miraculously resilient creature. Any appendage it loses, it eventually grows right back.

The shrimp—they like that, too.

\#

Casey tells me there's no one else. That I'm the only one, and I know it. She whines in her pathetic drunk girl voice, the one that makes her sound like she's from the Valley, even though there's not a hill around for a thousand miles. She whimpers and rolls her hips and says please.

I get up. Casey lays down. I do whatever Casey wants. The night heat breeds humidity between us. Her pale hair tides across my damp pillow in rogue waves like liquid moon.

She pulls down her cotton panties and spreads her plush knees.

She asks if I've ever done this before.

"Not the fingering part. Like, obviously. But with the tampon, I mean."

So I tell her about the woman who came into Our Lady when I was working gyno. She'd been having lower abdominal pain and thought she might need a pap smear about it. Her mother had just died. Cervical cancer at fifty.

Sometimes, you ignore a problem until you can't ignore the problem. Sometimes you let a thing fester until it's too late to fix.

This woman had a stink to her. At first, it was faint, like letters pressed into the next page, but once she tucked her knees up and stuck her feet in the stirrups, it bloomed. It was that kind of odor that lingers on you, even hours and days after, on your clothes and in your hair. A rotten you could taste with your mouth closed from across the room.

You expect a cunt to smell like one. It's healthy, even. Cunts should smell like cunts—not like spoiled meat from a deep freeze on the fritz. Not like funky iron and rancid flesh.

When the doctor swabbed the woman's cervix, it detached completely. It flaked away and fell right off. That's what he thought at first.

But no—inside this woman, what he'd actually found was a tampon, mashed up and compacted into a dark medallion. When he pulled it out, pus fountained up from the inflamed bud of her cervix, the color of movie theater popcorn butter. It flowed free and thick and *kept* flowing, on and on. I had to swoop in with a basin to try and catch it all, before it started puddling on the floor.

Imagine the smell then.

That tampon must have been in there for months. Years, maybe.

"Oh," the woman said when the doctor showed her. "I was wondering where that went."

#

Casey throws her head back and laughs the way a movie star does. She touches her face and rakes her fingers through her hair.

"Oh my god. That's awful. You're so fucking gross."

That's when I slide my fingers in.

Her pussy is fever hot and vice tight. Dry, or it would be, except for the blood. Thick, rubbery clots cling to my knuckles. Thin, stringy ones floss beneath my nails.

Casey's laughter breaks into panicked gasps.

"Okay, then. Just do it quick." Her eyes are fixed on the ceiling now. "Just get it out."

I shift onto my elbow for better leverage and probe deeper, fingers curled in a come hither.

I feel around for the tail of the little red mouse.

#

My ma and dad were professional shit-stirrers. They had a septic tank management business, a literal Mom and Pop. Their job was to crack tanks and break up blockages, pump out overflow. Maintain that delicate balance between solids, effluent, and scum.

People used to ask them how they could do something like that together. How they could spend whole days smelling other people's piss and shit, then come home reeking like piss and shit, and somehow keep their marriage alive.

"Maybe it's because we're in the thick of it together," Ma would say every time. She always said it like she'd never thought of it before. "His stink is my stink. Love is nose-blind."

Most of their emergency jobs were septic systems that weren't being used properly. Tanks full of cat litter or oven grease or buffet leftovers or even just hair. Work the system right, and it will maintain itself for years, but people screw it up without even thinking about it. It barely registers for them, where their discards go. It's cathartic, isn't it? Just shove it all down the drain.

When that happened, Dad would pop the tank and run the auger, which would break apart the crusty top layer. Ma would hold a flashlight and watch for interlopers. Anything that shouldn't have been in the tank, but was.

Disposable wipes were a big one. The rise of the moist towelette industry single-handedly funded my nursing degree. No matter what they say on the package, those wipes don't break down. Not ever. You can flush as many as you like, but they never really go away.

Another big one: tampons. From puberty to menopause, four or five every day, two to seven days a cycle, thirteen cycles a year—it adds up. They float on the surface in chain islands of blood logged cotton. Rat kings soaked in shredded womb.

Because of their color, and the strings trailing behind, Ma always called them little red mice.

One day, Ma and Dad got a call out to the old St. Mary's building. Fifty years ago, it was a boarding school for wayward girls, before the county shut it down. It sat vacant for decades until a developer finally bought the place, thinking they might turn it into a wedding venue or a prison. The septic system was completely shot. Given the building's history—all those women holed up together, bleeding in cycle synched stigmata—my folks were pretty sure they knew the cause.

Dad got to mixing. Ma held the flashlight. And sure enough, there they were—the mice.

But that wasn't all.

No one can prove it, not even Ma. The investigators went through the whole tank top to bottom after and didn't find anything. But she swears it to this day. She saw what she saw.

A tiny hand, flecked with fecal matter. A *baby's* hand, reaching up to them from the sewage smoothie abyss.

For just a whirl of the auger, it was there, reaching out like it wanted her to put her finger against its palm.

Then, it sank down into the rest of the refuse. Blended in. Disappeared.

#

"My grandma was a St. Mary's girl," Casey says.

"Yeah?" I wipe the sweat from my brow against her inner thigh. Casey always smells good, even now. She smells like vanilla and salt and wet earth.

"They did lobotomies there. Human experiments. Cult stuff. It was seriously fucked up. If your daughter got pregnant out of wedlock, or started running with the wrong crowd or just pissed you off, you shipped her there. Nine months later, she'd come home with a flat belly and cottage cheese for brains." Casey runs her hands down her stomach, rolling it out like enriched dough. "I was pregnant once."

The tendons in my hand crack, and the tampon string tickles my middle fingertip.

I tell her to lift her hips.

"It freaked me out. I don't know when it happened. I was partying pretty hard back then. Harder than I do now. I was actually thinking about keeping it—can you imagine? But then one day—"

"Casey?"

She sits up a little. "Yeah?"

"Just lift your hips."

She does, and the little cotton braid I've been probing for flicks down between my fingers.

"Got it." I clamp down on the tail. Casey goes stiff. "Just relax, okay? I'm gonna pull it out now."

Outside, something starts howling, high and wounded. I tell myself it's nothing. A drunk, maybe, or a dog. The wind.

"It's the weirdest thing," Casey whispers. "One day, I woke up, and it was just gone."

#

Last summer, the summer Casey broke the jalousie, she split up with her boyfriend. I never bothered learning his name. There was always a boyfriend, and Casey was always breaking up with him. I used to think she did it for fun.

This boyfriend, he had put her legs over his shoulders when they were fucking, then bent down to kiss her. It squished her stomach. She threw up in his mouth. He actually took it pretty well, until she told him to get out.

To get her mind off things, and because I had some news, we packed up my car and skipped town. I had enough money to cover us both for a couple of weeks. Casey wanted to drive until we hit the coast.

I meant to wait to tell her. I wanted to do it by the ocean, on the beach. But before we'd even cleared the hog confinements along the highway, it slipped out.

I told her I was going away.

"You're already away." Her feet were on the dash. She put her hand on my thigh. "You're away with me."

No, I told her. I was moving to the city. There was a girl. I'd met her online. She worked at the meat processing plant, picking over the offal, after all normal parts had been beefed and parceled off. She scooped out eyeballs, popped out testicles, removed cow vaginas from vulva to ovaries. It was rewarding work, she said. It felt honorable, using up every part. A restaurant downtown would buy these things and vacuum seal them with garlic and coriander seeds, then sous vide them low and slow until they fell apart in your hands.

The restaurant used them to make tacos. They served them with cilantro and pickled onion and lime.

"Oh, fuck off. You're not leaving," said Casey.

I said, yes, actually, I was.

"Fine." Her hand tightened on my thigh. She dropped her feet to the floor. "But if you go, you're *gone*. I won't even hate you. There won't be anything left to hate. I'll forget you, blank you out, put you from my mind. And someday, you'll see me in some restaurant or at the movies or pushing my cart at the Hy-Vee. And you'll push your cart over, hoping to God I might smile at you or say hi or even look your pathetic way. But I won't. I'll walk right past you like you're not there. Because you won't be. Not to me. To me, you never existed at all."

We never made it to the coast.

When I got back home, I locked the door behind me. I turned off my phone. For an hour, I stood in front of the bathroom mirror to make sure I was still standing there. Part of me, the part that Casey had, was just waiting to disappear.

It was a few days later when Casey kicked the slats out of the window. I don't think she even bothered calling or trying the front door. She climbed through the broken place, legs first, then arms, then the rest of her.

"Don't go," she whispered, curled up in bed next to me. "I need you. So just don't."

I do whatever Casey says.

#

I tug at the tampon. The string goes taut, but it doesn't budge.

"Hurry," Casey says. Her cunt clamps down on my fingers. She's breathing the way you do to blow a candle out. "I don't feel so good. This is getting weird."

I tell her to relax, and that I'm trying. I pull harder on the string, and finally, something gives.

It keeps giving.

First, my bloodstained fingers. Then, the tampon. It flops flaccid onto my bed sheets, bloated and dark.

"Is it out?" Casey asks, and I say yeah. It's out.

But that's not all.

There's something more. Something long and stringy, clinging to the tampon's tip. At first, I think it's a thick, ropy clot, and I dip my fingers beneath it to pull it free.

That's when I realize it's not blood.

It's *hair*.

Long hair. Dark hair. Brittle and elastic, the way Casey's gets when she fries it with too much bleach.

This is something that should faze me. But I've pulled worse things out of strangers. I've pulled Casey's hair from the depths of my drain and the crack of my ass. I'd do anything for Casey. That's love. That's *devotion*. What does this matter, compared to that?

"What's going on?" Casey asks. She's realized something's wrong.

I pull and keep pulling, hand over fist so it doesn't break off before it's free.

She sits up and sees what I'm doing.

"Stop it." She says it the way you'd talk to a dog. "Whatever you're doing to me, stop. Stop it right now."

The last of the hair slides out of her. But there's something else tangled up in its split ends.

There's a whole lot of something else.

A strand of pearls, every bead stained pink. Then, creeping vines, slim but sturdy, with globs of blood like crushed berries on their broad, flat leaves. Silk ribbon stained dark, yards and yards of it. Leather laces. Golden bells strung on a velvet cord. A rough, scratchy length of rope, looped off and tied in a hangman's knot. Crumbling silver tinsel, the kind you'd wreath around a Christmas tree. Antique lace. Twin sets of virgin blue rosary beads, entwined like snakes fucking. Racing down their decades, I spy tacky, fast-moving fur. Two actual little red mice, scurrying away.

It's too dark to see where they go.

Casey is sobbing now. She wants to know what's happening and why. Like I have an answer. I didn't put this shit inside of her. I'm only here to pull it out.

Casey calls me *you bitch*, then, *you fucking lezzie bitch,* as if any of that matters now.

Seaweed comes next with a rush of salt water. I hear the cries of gulls. The ocean, after all. Then, a length of barbed wire. It cuts into my palms as I grasp tight and pull harder. Impaled on its thorns, I find a severed finger, flesh sloughing away from bone. At its base, it still wears a gold wedding band.

I wonder whose it is.

I'm up to my elbow in Casey now. I can't remember when I pressed my hand inside. Casey has gone quiet, but she breathes when I do. Her heartbeat pulses around my forearm. My heart is beating to match.

In my fist inside Casey, there's a thin, cool chain. I'm convinced that if I can reach the end of it, I'll find a plug like the kind on a bathtub. I'll yank it out, and this will all go away.

"Hey," Casey rasps.

She says she's sorry for freaking out. She says everything is going to be okay. Everything will be okay now.

The chain slips through my fist and slithers free. There's nothing else on the other end.

"See?" I say. "It's over."

"Yeah," she says. "Must be."

I rest my head against Casey's belly. There's nothing in the world softer than her skin. We're swamped with sweat, but the room has gone cold.

I make a joke about how we'll joke about this someday. She laughs like when you run into someone, then run into them again trying to move aside. Her laughter clenches at my elbow and reverberates up to my funny bone. It reminds me that I'm still inside her.

I start to pull my arm out, but something catches me and holds me in. Pulls me deeper.

Slender, icy fingers, twining between mine.

#

When I first met Casey, it was in a bar. She told me not to fall in love with her. We shared lip gloss. I bought her a drink.

No one, it felt like, had ever really noticed me before. Not in the way she did. Not someone who looked like her.

I talked too much that night, and drank too much, which only made me talk even more. By closing time, I'd told her my entire life story and hadn't asked a single question.

Even now, years later, I still don't know Casey's parents' names, what they do, where they live. I couldn't tell you her first kiss, her first fuck, first love. I know she's an Aquarius sun, Cancer rising, but I don't know where Casey was born.

#

I'm on the floor of my bedroom, trembling. My knees are tucked against my chest. The cold is still there, burning in the places between my fingers, where whatever was inside Casey clasped its hand with mine.

Somewhere in the room, I think, Casey is here, too.

My eyes are closed. I keep them that way.

I wonder, when I open them, what I'll find.

Casey bleary-eyed and telling me to forget all of this, forget everything she's said; to please love her, to still love her, to find a way. Casey pulling her panties back on and collecting all the things I pulled out of her, gathering them up in her arms and leaving through the door. A starfish with four arms, dragging itself out of Casey's pussy and slouching off somewhere dark and safe to regrow. An empty bed, soaked in no one's sweat but my own, like she never existed at all.

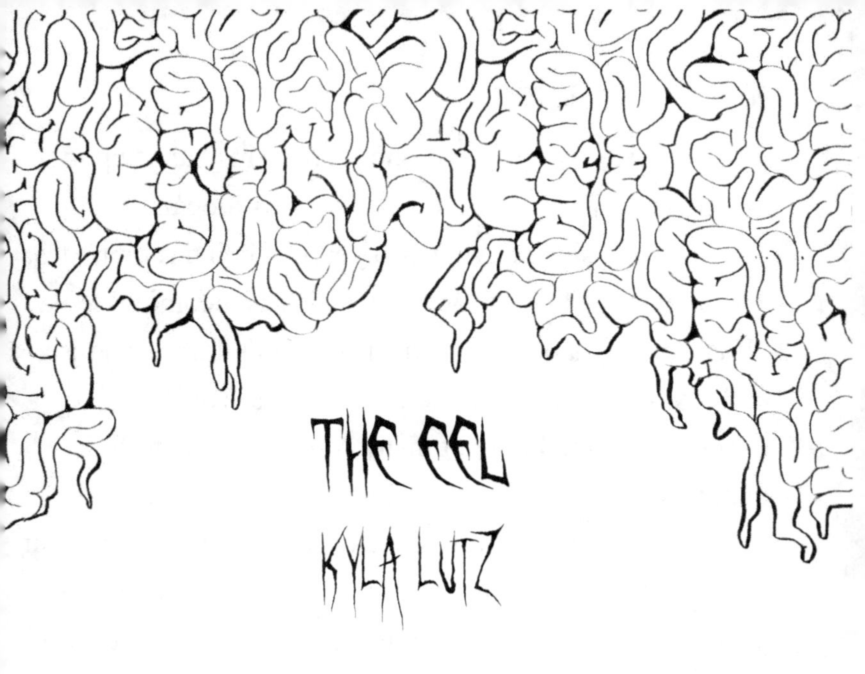

THE EEL
KYLA LUTZ

"Are you sure this is going to work?"

Claes didn't look up, pushing the sharp point of the needle through the fat worm squirming between his fingertips. Claes sent it towards the end of the line, where half a dozen worms already sat impaled and writhing. "Yes," he finally answered, blue eyes flitting up to meet Jake's dark ones. "This will work."

"You know, when I asked you to show me something Swedish, I was expecting fjords or meatballs or—"

"*This* is what I think of as Swedish." He gestured around them, from his grandfather's small cottage to the stream that ran about twenty feet from where they sat. "Not the stereotypes."

"Okay, okay," Jake said, putting his hands up in surrender. "I just thought eel fishing was illegal."

Claes sighed. After two years of being roommates, Jake recognized it as Claes's 'a lecture is incoming' look. "It is," he explained. "But this is my grandfather's house, and it's where he taught me to catch eels. You'll get to experience something not many Americans get to experience. One eel won't kill anyone."

"Famous last words," Jake said, but he reached out and took the fishing line, snipping off a length similar to the one Claes was using. For the next few minutes they worked in silence, threading worm after worm onto the line, the wriggling balls at the end growing larger and larger.

Jake hated it. The smell of them, the look of them, the way they moved… if he hadn't been so touched that Claes had brought him out here, he never would have agreed to this worm massacre. He threaded another, trying not to think about it. They were *worms*, they didn't feel pain, but as the worm ball grew larger the repetitive impalement became more disturbing. What if some alien creature yanked him out of his bed and tossed him in a bucket only to impale him with a needle and slide him, skewered, into a slimy, stinking mass of other humans?

"I think it's big enough," Claes said, looking at the worm ball Jake was working on.

"So, uh, we just go out on the boat and fish with these like normal?" Jake asked, looking at the setting sun, nervous with anticipation. Did Sweden have eel-fishing police?

"Not exactly," Claes told him. "I think it's easier to show you than it is to try and explain it." He lifted both lines and set them into the now-empty bucket they'd kept their collected worms in, getting to his feet. "Let's go."

"Sure thing," Jake grabbed the bucket and started heading to the stream. It was more like a river, and only a few miles in from the sea. The eels swam in, headed up to wherever eels lived, and then swam back out when some internal clock told them it was time to head back to the ocean. Instinct really was a weird fucking thing.

"Ready?" Claes asked, appearing at his shoulder with a pair of oars. The row boat was rickety but still safe, and they got it into the water without issue. Claes stopped them once he'd rowed about fifty feet up the stream. He reached over to the bucket and removed his cluster of worms, gesturing for Jake to do the same. "Keep hold of the end of your line and toss them in the water."

Jake did as he was told, watching the worms as they sank out of sight. They settled against the riverbed and moved to pull them up a little before Claes stopped him. "Don't," he said. "The trick is to leave them on the bottom in the silt. The eels come because of how the worms move, and when you feel a tug, you can pull them up. The movement makes the eels bite down and get trapped."

"Really? We don't, like… lure them in?"

"No. With *klumma* the eels do the work for us. It may take a while, but they'll bite." Claes shifted on his seat, peering down into the steadily darkening water. "When there were more eels, you could hardly pull them up fast enough. They would just bite and bite until the boat was full."

A boat full of eels fighting to get back into the water. It sounded like hell. Jake frowned, keeping a loose grip on his line. It seemed impossible that the eels would just find the worms, bite that horrible mass of pink flesh on their own. "And now?"

"We'll catch a few," Claes said. "Obviously we don't need them like we used to, but I like the taste. We can cook whatever we catch for breakfast." He looked at Jake, smiling. "I hope you like the taste of them, too."

A surge of affection struck Jake. Claes had gone to all this trouble to show him a slice of Nordic life, an experience most Americans could never hope to have, and Jake wasn't going to forget that anytime soon. They sat in companionable silence for a while, the only sound the water lapping gently at the side of the boat. It would be so easy to fall asleep out here and he might have even begun to doze when Claes spoke again, soft and pensive. "You know, they still don't know much about how eels breed."

"Really?" Jake asked. "That's kind of crazy. How do they not know?"

"It's strange, right?" Claes said. He looked over at Jake, his face illuminated only by the moonlight, flashlight-under-his-chin spooky in the dim light. "The eels go back to the Sargasso Sea once they're adults, but scientists lose track of them at some point. Then all these babies appear, but they've never seen an adult in the Sargasso Sea. Just the little ones."

Jake thought about how insane that seemed. The eels came all the way here just to go *back* to Bermuda? "What's the point? Coming all the way here just to turn around and go back a few years later? It's fucking weird."

Claes nodded, the boat rocking as he moved to look over the edge into the star-dappled water. "My grandfather always said that the eels come here for some reason, even if we can't understand it. This is where they undergo the transformation that tells them they need to breed."

"You should be an eel scientist," Jake said, rolling his shoulders to shake out a cramp forming in his shoulder blade. As soon as he did that, however, he felt a tug at the line. He froze, staring down at his hand, convinced he'd imagined it until the tug came again, more insistent. "Holy shit," he said, any instructions Claes had given him completely forgotten. "It moved!"

"Don't panic," Claes, half-laughed as he reached out, grasping the line alongside Jake. He tugged on it, looking pleased at the weight. "Yeah, I think you've got one! Okay, come on, let's haul it in."

"How?"

"Just grab the line with me and we'll yank it up."

Jake nodded, wrapping his fingers around the line alongside Claes. The eel was squirming on the other end, thrashing against the pull, and as they hauled the eel briefly broke the surface, its long, muscular tail slapping against the water and sending droplets bursting up over the pair. It was bigger than he'd expected, a few feet long, and adrenaline surged through Jake as he pulled harder on the line.

They finally got it into the boat, slick black body thumping against the wood. Claes dropped the line and grabbed their bucket, dunking it in the stream to fill it with water. Jake steeled himself before grabbing the tail of the eel, the muscle pulsing against his fingers before he managed to yank it from the floorboards, shoving it in the bucket.

"Oh my god," he gasped, peering into the frothing water before lifting his gaze back to Claes. "We're gonna need a bigger bucket." Claes stared at him, frowning, and Jake sighed. "*Jaws*? The shark movie?"

"*Hajen*," Claes said, waving his hand. "Okay, yes. I know now. Not a very good joke."

"It was a great joke." Jake stared at the eel; it was a mass of black flesh and slime, whipped into a terrible frenzy and nearly too big for the five-gallon bucket they'd gotten from the hardware store. "Are they usually this big?"

Claes didn't answer. He was peering at the bucket, his own *klumma* long forgotten after the excitement of catching this eel. Jake's hands were covered in fish slime and water along with a small trickle of blood—his palm had been cut. He sat back on his seat, adrenaline still coursing through him. "Claes. Answer the question. It seems big."

"It is," Claes said, his voice far away, distracted. "We came to find yellow eels."

"That eel is *not* yellow," Jake said, stating the obvious.

The thing had to be at least three and a half feet long, about the diameter of a human fist, and, although Jake couldn't get a good look at its head now, the jaw had appeared hooked and wicked. "Dude, what the fuck kind of eel is that?"

"I've seen this kind, once before," Claes said, moving mechanically. He put the lid on the bucket and the darkness seemed to help calm it down somewhat, the creature not thrashing as much. "We won't need a second eel. This one will be enough for us, I think."

"You seem scared," Jake wrung his hands out to try and work off some of the nerves. "It's freaking me out."

"No, don't be worried," Claes told him, but Jake felt just the opposite. "Sorry. I haven't seen one of these since I was a child. It reminded me of my grandfather. It's strange to miss him because of an eel, I guess."

They both went silent, Jake looking at everything except Claes, and Claes looking at the bucket. They were silent as they rowed back to the dock, with Claes pulling on the oars and Jake watching the bucket, still in the bottom of the boat. It didn't take them long, the natural drift of the stream having done most of the work for them, and Claes navigated them deftly to the shore, purposefully grounding the row boat before climbing out. Jake clambered after him and helped grab the bucket, now too heavy for just one of them with the added water and eel inside.

They carried it to the small stone shed that sat on the property, Claes briefly setting the eel down to get the door open.

"What's in here?" Jake asked, and Claes pushed the door open enough for him to see: a trench dug in the floor, filled with a couple feet of water that glistened from a single lightbulb that hung overhead, and a line of racks on the right side. "Is this shed just for eels?"

"Mostly," Claes said, gesturing for him to help with the bucket again. They got the eel to the trench and tipped it into the water; the creature thrashed and roiled for a few moments, and when it finally settled, Claes turned to Jake. "Well, we'll have quite the feast tomorrow," he sighed, some of the life coming back to him. "I think we deserve a reward."

"Vodka?"

"Vodka." Claes agreed, trudging out of the shed and closing the door once Jake had followed him out, leading him back to the main house. "It's tradition. Or, at least, my family's tradition. Sit down and I'll pour us some."

Jake groaned as he settled down in the living room, glad to be done with the physical labor. "So, what kind of eel is that?"

"I'm not sure," Claes admitted, voice slightly muffled from the distance between them. "I only know the name of the yellow eels." He reappeared, sitting across from Jake and handing him a small glass of vodka before raising his own. "Skål," he said, downing his drink.

Jake did the same, grinning at Claes. "I'm glad you brought me to do that. Honestly, I was kind of grossed out but it was still fun. I can't believe the fucking size of that thing!"

Claes leaned forward and rested his elbow on his knee, the intensity in his eyes something Jake was unaccustomed to. "You know you've been a good friend to me, Jake."

"I know," Jake felt a chill going up the back of his neck. What a weird thing to say out of the blue. "I feel the same way about you."

"There's been times when I've felt… differently about you," Claes continued. "Romantic."

Jake's mouth went dry. "And?"

"It makes me sad about what has to happen here tonight."

Jake stared at him, his smile fading slightly. "What does that mean?"

"Can you do me a favor?" Claes asked. "Can you try to move your right arm?"

Jake tried to do as he was told but, found that he couldn't; no matter how much he concentrated, his right arm would not raise off the couch. His eyes darted towards Claes. "Claes, what did you do?"

"Did I ever tell you how my father died?" Claes asked, ignoring the question. He leaned forward, peering at Jake intently. "Why I was raised by my grandfather? I don't think I did." He pushed to his feet and walked over, sliding an arm under his knees as he lifted Jake easily in a bridal hold.

"Claes," Jake said weakly, head lolling back uncontrollably as he was pulled into Claes's arms, heart thumping in his chest. "You don't have to do this."

"Please don't beg," Claes said. "We should go about this with dignity, Jake. I didn't suspect this would happen… but it has, and we both have our roles to play as a result."

He shouldered the back door of the house open, padding barefoot down the back steps towards the eel shed. "You shouldn't feel pain, at least. The paralytic I gave you is quite strong."

"Why did you bring a paralytic?" Jake mumbled, his words beginning to slur. "Did you plan this? Did you bring me here just to do this?"

"No," Claes readjusted his grip on Jake as he pushed the door to the shed open. The eel in the water flailed as they entered, Claes making a soft soothing noise before laying Jake on the cold stone floor. He crouched beside him, face hidden in the dim light. "The paralytic was just in case. I really did bring you here to share my culture, Jake. I just regret that I have to share more of it than I intended."

Claes straightened up, reaching towards the ceiling of the shed, above the dark water where the eel lurked. Jake tried to focus on what he was grasping for, but it was too far, and his stomach churned and his mouth went sour with fear. Claes pulled two meat hooks on chains down from the ceiling, the ends of them honed sharp. Claes crouched alongside him, sighing softly. "Please," he said, hooking a hand in the front of Jake's shirt and hoisting him into a sitting position, Jake falling forward, stopped only by Claes's shoulder. "Don't look at me like. You'll understand soon enough."

Jake, his cheek smushed against Claes's shoulder, stared past him to the door of the shed, the watery, dim light of the single bulb bleeding out onto the grass beyond. "What happened to your dad?" he asked, voice muffled against the fabric of his sweater.

Claes's fingers, cool and soft, were at the hem of his shirt. He hesitated, and Jake could feel his heart beating, calm and collected against the rabbit-fast thrum of Jake's own. It took Claes only a moment to recover, pulling Jake's shirt over and off his head. Unable to stop it from happening, he felt like a rag doll being undressed by an overzealous owner. He nearly fell backwards again until Claes caught him, pressing his fingers into Jake's shoulder blade; for a moment, Jake wondered what he was doing until he realized his roommate was palpating for the space between his spine and his scapula. "Claes…"

"It won't hurt you the way it hurt my father," Claes murmured. He dragged a chain across the stone, an unbearable pressure pushing against Jake's skin. Jake *knew* the hook was slipping into the soft spot Claes had discovered. The hook scraped against bone, and, for a few moments, Jake thought maybe the pain would have been better than the unbearable pressure of dry hook against wet bone.

He'd been told not to beg—but Jake had never been great at keeping his mouth shut. "Please, man, this… it's not beyond repair, okay?"

"It was over as soon as you caught that eel," Claes said plainly, pulling back from Jake and looking him in the eyes. There was sorrow there but determination, too, and Jake realized he had no leverage here. He should have recognized the wrongness of the situation as soon as Claes had gone so quiet. "There's nothing to repair here. You've done nothing wrong."

He stood up and Jake slumped forward, kept upright only by the hooks in his back, pulling on the bone and digging deeper into the flesh. Claes stepped out of sight and Jake began to be dragged backwards, his body rasping over the stone. Pulled into a poor facsimile of standing, his toes barely touching the stone floor, Claes continued to tug on the rudimentary crank attached to the chains until Jake was fully suspended above the water.

Reappearing in his peripheral, standing on the very brink of the trench, Claes undid Jake's jeans. "I'm sorry," he said. "I know this isn't very dignified—but it's necessary. There have to be the proper points of egress."

"Jesus Christ," Jake whispered. *Egress*? What a fucking horrifying thing to be told. What else could Claes be talking about but egress for *that thing*?

Jake's boxers came next, leaving him nude and hanging like so much meat. "I'll begin soon, once I'm sure the paralytic has reached full effect," Claes told him, sitting down at the water's edge and dragging his hand through it, the eel staying quiet. "You asked about my father. I was seven the last time I saw one of these," he said. "My grandfather and father took me out. I never liked fishing using *klumma*. I thought it was too dirty—but my grandfather loved it, swore by it. We only ever caught yellow eels, but that day we caught one of *these*. I don't think they have a name, at least, not one I know. But they have always existed, and we have always held this obligation to them."

He paused for a moment, looking up at Jake. "My father was the one who caught the eel. He brought it on board and my grandfather grew quiet. They both knew what would come. He was brought to this shed and he was hung by his shoulders and he…" Claes trailed off. "Well, you'll see. I wish this hadn't happened. My grandfather told me that the eels often ask for the ones we love, but I didn't think… it's too late now. No time for regret."

He plunged his hands into the water and pulled out the eel, squirming and writhing in his grasp but unable to break free. Despair gripped Jake, so intense and so terrible that he couldn't even bring himself to scream. Claes straddled the trench, body pressed close to Jake with the eel squirming between them. He hoisted the eel up in one arm, pinning it to his chest, and reached up with his other hand, taking Jake's chin in his hand. Whatever Claes saw in Jake's eyes didn't even make him pause before he plunged two fingers between his lips and forced his jaw open.

Jake had no time to react before the head of the eel was being forced into his mouth. It was slick and bitter, tasted of silt and mud, and he couldn't even close his eyes as his best friend shoved the writhing creature deeper and deeper. Once past his teeth, the eel began to move on its own, pulsing forward into his throat, past his gag reflex and down into his esophagus. Claes's careful mask was slipping—he was staring with open fascination, the eel halfway inside Jake, muscles pushing against him from the inside. He tried to scream around the thing. Claes put a hand on his arm; what had once been soothing was now terribly cold.

With an awful squelching, the eel slid all the way in. Jake screamed, this time unfettered and *loud*, but Claes just moved away from him, closing the door to the shed. Jake hung there, alone, body immobilized, mouth full of slime and what he suspected was blood from his ruined throat. It was all dripping down his chest, plinking into the water and sending ripples through it, and for a moment everything was still.

And then Jake felt it split.

"Oh my god, oh my god," he whispered. He could feel it writhing, but not the same as before; instead of one strong eel pressing against his organs, it now felt like a thousand, a *million*. "What did you do to me?!"

"We don't know how eels breed," Claes said calmly. "Or, I suppose… *Scientists* don't know how eels breed. I do. They need a warm, dark space, Jake. What better than a human stomach to meet those parameters?"

They were everywhere now. Jake knew they were no longer contained to his stomach; there was no pain—but he could *feel* them, squirming around his insides, finding their way through his intestines, his organs, his…

Something was pressing against the back of his eyes. Pressure was building, little black spots appearing in his vision, and suddenly he could see something squirming in the inner corner of his eye. "Oh, this happened to my father, too." Claes said, like he was taking notes at a clinical study. "The glass eels, the little ones… They find all these little exits that you and I wouldn't think of."

Jake watched as the twisting little thing grew longer, transparent and wriggling, until it freed itself completely and fell into the water. A noise, animal and tortured, came tearing from his throat, but it was quickly cut off as he gagged, vomiting a clump of glass eels into the water below. *"Claes…"*

"It shouldn't last too much longer," Claes soothed. "Once they reach your eyes, the brain isn't far behind."

The eels were taking strange new paths through his body. They were falling with more vigor now, rain drops into the enclosure, and he wished he could fucking cry—but instead of tears there were eels dripping down his face; from his eyes, his nose, his mouth. A popping sound followed by deafness in his left ear. The black spots were growing larger, bleeding together, obscuring huge chunks of his vision, but Claes still watched him.

The pressure against the back of his eyes was enormous. Something gave—his right eye went dark, a rush of baby eels splattering into the water below. Jake, strangled and hoarse, screamed as he saw what was floating in the water alongside the eels: an eyeball, *his* eyeball, forced from his skull by the unyielding mass of a million little eels.

It didn't take much longer for him to lose the last of his hearing, the last of his sight, the only sensation the continued pressure between his shoulder blades and the incessant squirming in every last inch of his body. They were among his organs, under his skin, within every last crevice.

Claes was right about one thing, though; after his eyes went, it didn't take long for the eels to reach his brain.

They brought the girl in around 5 AM. Anderson had been shooting the shit with some of the officers at the front desk, but all chatter ceased the moment they saw the gore streaking down the hysterical young woman's face. The others had balked away, but Tim Anderson, who never missed an opportunity to look good in front of his colleagues, didn't hesitate to rush forward and take the girl's shoulder to support her weight.

"What's wrong?" he asked sharply, looking at the troopers who had brought her in. "Is she hurt?"

"Not her blood," answered the trooper. Sergeant Duran had heard the commotion in the precinct lobby and came out of her office. She took the trembling girl from Anderson and nodded to another female officer, Diaz, to help her bring the girl to the ladies' room so she could clean up.

While they were occupied, Anderson asked the troopers everything they knew. He had aspirations of making Detective before he turned 30, and although his night shift was almost up, intuition told him this was not a case he wanted to miss.

The troopers had identified the girl as Eileen Carr, 24. She was a student at the nearby University of New Mexico. No prior arrests or history of mental illness. They had been patrolling up the 40 when they'd spotted her on the side of the road, covered in what looked like blood and bodily fluid, sobbing hysterically. After determining that she wasn't injured, they'd calmed her down enough to consent to a ride to the nearest station.

When Carr was ready to talk, Anderson slipped into Interview Room 2 and joined Diaz and Duran. He knew that Duran likely felt he didn't need to be there, that she and Diaz had it covered. But his interest was piqued, and he also knew that Duran wouldn't interrupt the interview just to kick him out. *Besides,* he thought, *this is police work. There ought to be at least one man in the room.*

"OK, honey," Duran said, using a maternal voice that Anderson knew to be wholly artificial, "Can you tell us what happened?"

"My brother," the girl moaned, "He's dead, he's dead, it's all my fault…"

The look on her face was familiar; Anderson had seen it from those who survived particularly nasty car crashes. She was still trembling, and Diaz took off her jacket and draped it over the younger woman's shoulders. Carr leaned forward and held her temples in both hands, pushing her hair back against her head. "Oh, god, *Connie*..."

"Why don't you start at the beginning," Duran suggested gently, folding her hands over the desk like a school principal. "It's alright. Everything's going to be OK."

The look in her eyes suggested Eileen Carr didn't believe that for a hot second… but she began to tell them, anyway.

The Carr siblings lived together at the Twinside Apartments in Netherwood Park, a few miles north of the UNM main campus. Eileen was the older of the two, a Psych major in her second year of grad school. Her brother Conrad was a junior-year Communications student, and, according to Eileen, not doing well at it. "Our mom died last year," Eileen explained, dabbing at her eyes. "Connie took it pretty hard. He's always had trouble with, like, ADHD, but it got really bad after… it just got bad."

The trouble had started, Eileen said, with a package she'd found on their apartment doorstep. It was a small box, made of glossy black cardboard, lacking any postage or identifying information. The box made her nervous;

she'd been about to throw it out without even opening it, but she'd decided to ask Conrad if he'd been expecting a package.

"I wish I hadn't," she said in a hollow voice. "I should have just thrown it away."

The package was his, and although he'd been reluctant to tell her what was in it, she'd eventually pried it out of him. The unmarked box contained a single bottle of pills. There was no prescription information, no doctor's signature, which concerned Eileen greatly.

"It's a free trial from some pharmaceutical company," Conrad had offered. "I saw it on Reddit. They're supposed to help increase focus, impulse control, that kind of thing."

"I tried to tell him it was a bad idea," Eileen said miserably. "The whole thing seemed sketchy from the start, but he didn't want to listen. We'd been fighting a lot about his grades, and his internet friends kept telling him how safe it was…"

The argument had ended, like so many before it, with Conrad storming into his room and slamming the door shut. He'd become something of a hermit over the last year, Eileen told them. She was worried about her brother, but what could she do? She wasn't their mom; she had no authority to punish him. Nor could she bring herself to kick him out of the apartment, even though he was 3 months behind on their shared rent. With their mother gone, the siblings were the only family each other had left.

At this, Eileen burst into a fresh bout of tears. While Duran consoled her, Anderson exchanged a glance with Diaz: *Jesus, lady, get to the fucking point already.*

After blowing her nose, Eileen continued. The pills, she said, had an almost immediate improvement on both Conrad's grades and his mood. More than once she would come home from work to find him on the couch on his laptop, textbooks splayed over the coffee table. When she spoke to him, he was active, engaged, alert. He asked her questions about her Psych program, her own studies. Once she had even come home to find him poring over *her* textbooks.

"Are you planning to switch majors or something?" she'd asked.

"Nah." He lowered the textbook and smiled up at her, and for just a moment she saw the boy he'd been, the bright-eyed little brother who used to hold her hand when they walked to the bus stop together. "I finished my assignment early and was looking for something to read. This stuff is really interesting!"

They'd then fallen into a conversation about psychology that lasted at least an hour, during which Eileen was pleasantly shocked at just how well her brother kept up. It was like talking to a fellow grad student, not someone who'd just cracked open the book for the first time that afternoon. "I made a joke about *Flowers for Algernon* at some point," she recalled. Anderson didn't understand the reference, but Diaz and Duran only nodded.

So it had been good, for a while. Eileen couldn't bring herself to exactly *approve* of Conrad ordering some shady "miracle intelligence pill" online, but she allowed her worries to quietly fade into the background. Conrad was happy. His grades were improving. He even paid his half of the rent.

And then it started going wrong.

Conrad got sick, Eileen said. He played it off as just a cold, but the walls in their apartment weren't so thin that she couldn't hear him throwing up in the bathroom, even when he ran the shower at night. His skin was clammy and strangely cold, though he was sweating through his clothes. After a few days of this, she'd begged her brother to see a doctor, but he wouldn't hear it. Instead, he shut himself in his room, citing illness to his professors and continuing his coursework online.

Eileen's anxiety about the pills had returned in full force. "I made him promise to stop taking them for a while," she recounted, "and he agreed, but I think he was lying. I know because I snuck into his room once when he was in the shower. I checked the bottle. More pills were missing, and this was *after* he told me he'd stop."

That was when she'd first noticed the smell. Conrad's room had never smelled *great*; he kept a pet bearded dragon named Jazz, and while he claimed that he cleaned her tank once a week, Eileen had always detected a faintly arid, leathery stink from it. As she spent little time in Conrad's room, it was easy enough to ignore.

The new smell was different. It was greasy, oily, somehow *chemical.* It grew stronger as she approached his bed. The comforter and sheets were soaked with something, some thick fluid. She reached out a finger to touch whatever it was—

—but then she'd heard the shower stop, and she'd bolted from the room before Conrad could notice her entry.

Another week passed, and Eileen saw almost nothing of her brother. She spent most of her days out of the house, at the college, or work, but that Saturday she stayed home to look after him. When Eileen knocked to ask if he needed anything, he told her he was napping, and to leave him alone.

At his door, she'd noticed the smell again. It was faint, but it was there.

Con stayed shut away in his room for the rest of that day; it was around 11 PM when she finally heard his door open and his footsteps shuffling out. The moment she heard him emerge, she immediately left her room to check on him.

What she saw nearly stopped her heart.

Conrad was emaciated. He was wearing a ratty old t-shirt that hung off of him like a garbage bag; she could see the outline of his spine pressed against the fabric as he bent to pick something out of the fridge. The kitchen was dark, but in the light of the refrigerator she could see how pale his skin was: the color of a corpse on the autopsy table. In the span of a week, her brother had wasted away.

An involuntary gasp slipped out, prompting Conrad to turn and face her—and for just a moment, Eileen's horror turned to confusion. Absurdly, she thought Connie was wearing a Halloween mask; some kind of bizarre prank, like the ones he'd pulled on her in their teenage years.

But it wasn't a mask. Conrad's skull appeared to be *swollen*, Eileen told the officers. She'd thought there was something wrong with his eyes at first; it took a few seconds for her to realize that they were being crowded *down*, pushed into a squint by the weight of his bulging forehead. She saw a vein worming down his right temple. He was missing hair in patches; the pale bald spots stood out against his dark, uncombed mane like sandbars in a night tide.

"Connie," she whispered, "what's happening to you?"

"What do you mean?" her brother asked, and in his piggishly flat eyes she saw genuine curiosity. "I feel *great*."

He'd smiled; a sick grin that felt almost painted on. Then he'd walked nonchalantly toward her. She cringed away with a little shriek, but he'd brushed past her without a second glance. Eileen saw that he was still sweating, but it seemed like…

The girl was struggling with her words here. Eventually she settled on: "It didn't look like sweat. It looked like *slime*. Like his skin was covered in…" Eileen covered her own forehead with one hand. She seemed embarrassed. "Look, I—I know how insane it sounds. But I'm telling you, it's what I saw."

Anderson didn't doubt it. If the girl was tweaking too, which he strongly suspected she had been, there was no end to the crazy shit she might have hallucinated. He'd once arrested a junkie who had taken a shaving razor to his own arms, flaying the skin off in rags to get rid of the "maggots" he saw writhing there.

"I almost called you guys then," Eileen continued, "but there was something I wanted to try first."

Whatever the substance was on Conrad's skin, she said, he'd left some of it behind on his snack run. The handle of the refrigerator door was coated in slimy, translucent gunk where he'd grabbed it. It smelled the way his sheets had. If Con hadn't been wearing socks, Eileen thought, he would have left footprints of the stuff where he walked. The image made her gag.

She'd scraped some of the stuff off into a plastic baggie, and after a fitful, sleepless night, she'd taken it to the science lab at the university and asked if they could identify it. She knew it was stupid, but she thought maybe if they could figure out what was wrong with Conrad, give her a solid diagnosis, she might be able to convince him to see a doctor. "Or at least make him throw out the fucking pills," she muttered.

It was a waste of time. The professor she'd spoken to hadn't been able to identify the substance. "It looks like cerebrospinal fluid," he said, "but it's full of digestive acids you'd normally find in bile. Where did you say you found this?"

Eileen's fears were stoked, and she found herself unable to return to the apartment. What if Conrad came out again, still sweating that weird sludge? What if he *touched* her? Shame filled Eileen's voice as she spoke. "I didn't know what to do. I called my friend Kira and asked if I could spend the night with her. I was so tired, so scared... I just wanted to sleep."

It was past midnight when she finally woke up. The rest had been good for her. The fear was still there, but it was no longer all-consuming; her mind felt clear. Clear enough to move forward, at least.

Something was horribly wrong with her brother. She was certain that those fucked-up Dark Web pills were responsible. Eileen was the older sister; it was her job to protect him, and she was failing. She had to fix it, if she could. She had to go back.

That had been four hours ago.

Eileen had returned to the apartment, one hand gripped tightly around the small canister of pepper spray she kept in her purse. She'd never had to use it before, and never in a million years had she imagined having to use it on *Connie*. But the memory of his cold, terrible smile

—*I feel* **great**—

Stuck in her like a splinter.

It had taken all her courage to open the front door of the apartment, and even more to knock on Conrad's bedroom door. There was no answer. She tried again, called his name.

Nothing.

Oh my dear God, he's dead in there. Eileen felt that, if she opened the door to find her brother's corpse lying in bed, there was a strong chance she might just go insane. But she couldn't bring herself to turn back, either. For one hellish moment she just stood there, in front of his bedroom, and then somehow her hand raised and she opened the door.

The smell was bad, but it was *nothing* compared to what she saw.

The slime was everywhere. It coated the walls, the furniture, Jazz's tank, even Conrad's beloved computer. The entire room was slick with a layer of gossamer jelly, like some mad painter had gone to work with a gallon-sized tub of Vaseline. A swell of the stuff was slowly oozing down the back wall.

There was just enough light coming in from the hallway for Eileen to see something lying on the floor a few feet in front of her. She dared not touch it, but some insane urge made her step forward and crouch. She couldn't make out what it was, and so, with trembling fingers she tapped the flashlight on her phone.

It was Jazz. The little lizard's head was gone, and the rest of its body lay on the floor like discarded trash. The corpse glistened with the same thick fluid that flooded the rest of the room.

Something in Eileen broke then. She staggered back, about to flee, when a voice croaked from Conrad's bathroom. "*Lee,*" it called, low and rasping. "*Lee, is that you?*"

I can't go in there, she thought, *I can't see him. I'll scream.* It was as if her legs hadn't gotten the message— Numbly, they carried her forward into the dripping, reeking hell that Conrad's room had become. She felt the wet carpet squish beneath her shoes, pictured herself slipping and falling head first into the stuff, and her throat clenched.

Cringing, she used the tip of her sneaker to push the bathroom door open, and shone her light upon the thing her brother had become. Eileen *did* scream when she finally saw him. A single, shrill shriek escaped her lips before she shoved her hands against her mouth and howled between her fingers.

Conrad was lying naked in the tub, a skin-wrapped skeleton. His muscles and body mass had faded away to nothing. Even his cheeks were sunken and wan, sucked dry of all vitality. But that wasn't what had made Eileen scream.

Her brother's skull had swollen to an obscene size. It rested against the slant of the bathtub's edge and the wall, as if Conrad's head was too heavy for him to hold it upright. His hair was completely gone; it had fallen out in clumps that lay littered around the upper half of the tub. But she could see more of those nestled veins, throbbing almost hungrily against the taut, straining skin of his scalp.

"*Lee*," he breathed. She could barely see his eyes, crushed as they were beneath the weight of his oversized forehead. But what little she *could* see of them was looking back at her. "Help me, Lee. Help me…"

"Con… Oh my god…" Eileen inched closer. Part of her wanted nothing more than to reach forward and take her brother's hand. Another, perhaps much a larger part of her was screaming— *the lizard, the lizard's head was gone*—at her to run away. Tears began to streak down her face. "You're gonna… you're gonna be OK…" she said weakly. "I-I'm gonna get you help, Connie, OK? It's going to be OK…"

"Lee…" he whimpered, and a fresh lance of heartbreak stabbed her through the chest. He sounded so sick, so hurt, so pathetic. Eileen hated herself for her fear, her revulsion, her weakness. His squished eyes were pleading with her. "Lee, I'm so… I'm so…"

She had bent over the tub, ignoring the stink, ignoring her horror, intent on taking his hand one last time. Giving him what comfort she could in this impossible nightmare. And that was when his face lit up, and she realized his eyes weren't afraid, weren't pleading for help, they were—

"HUNGRYYYYYYY!" Conrad screeched, and the entire mass of his mountainous skull swung towards her. His bony hands rose to grab her by the back of her head; his wet fingers digging into her hair as he tried to pull her forward towards his own shrieking mouth.

Eileen had no conscious control over what happened next. Pure instinct drove her backwards, tearing against Conrad's grip and pulling him with her away from the tub. It happened in an instant. His bulging skull swung over the tub's edge, and she could feel the immense *weight* of it, like a wrecking ball on a chain, heavy, *too heavy*—

Her brother's neck snapped like a tree branch. His face swung over the edge of the tub and then smashed against it comically. The entire heaving mass exploded on impact, a firework of flesh and fluid. Eileen was showered with a wave of viscera; she tasted a hot, pulpy mass in her screaming mouth, like copper-flavored chili. She couldn't see. Her eyes were covered in the steaming effluvia that had once been her brother's head.

"What happened then?" Duran asked.

"I ran," Eileen choked out through a sob. "I just… ran. They brought me here. And Con, he's… he's still back there."

By the time she'd finished her story, dawn was only a few hours away. They'd left the girl in the interview room to collect herself while Duran pulled Anderson and Diaz aside. "Alright. Wilder parts of her story aside, I think it's pretty clear the girl's brother is in a bad way."

The sergeant tasked Anderson and Diaz with checking out the apartment. Anderson was quietly thrilled; however it shook out, the Case of the Evil Brain Pills would look good on his resume next time he applied for Homicide. He imagined himself recounting the girl's story to the other detectives, laughing as he imitated Carr's expression when her brother's head "exploded" on her face.

They pulled up at Twinside, parked their patrol car on the street and headed inside. Rather than one large tower, the complex was made up of several smaller two-story buildings, with each floor containing several units. Carr had mentioned that she and her brother were the only tenants on their floor, which explained how things had gotten as bad as they had without the neighbors noticing.

Even still, as the officers ascended the exterior staircase leading up to the Carr siblings' apartment, Anderson was taken aback by the strength of the stench.

Christ, that reeks! Even if the Carr girl hadn't come weeping into the station, it wouldn't have been long before someone had called in an odor nuisance. He saw that the apartment's front door was open; Carr must not have closed it when she'd come stumbling out in a shell-shocked fugue.

Anderson and Diaz glanced at each other; she'd unbuttoned her blouse and was using her t-shirt to cover her nose. *You first,* her eyes said. He rapped his knuckles against the open door and called out, ignoring the lump in his throat. "APD! Anybody home?"

He didn't expect a response and didn't receive one. Without waiting to consult Diaz, Anderson stepped over the threshold; with the girl's story, they had more than enough grounds for probable cause to enter. *Besides, the door's wide fucking open.*

Diaz must not have disagreed, because she followed him in and called out herself: "Conrad Carr? You in here?" Hearing no answer, Anderson flicked the light switch. It was dead. He unbuckled his flashlight, swept it over the living room—

—and saw it. The brother's bedroom, his door wide open. And goddamned if it wasn't reflecting the light back at him. The interior of the room was oily and dank, like the walls of an underground sea-cave. Just as the girl had described.

"Diaz," he murmured, "what the hell am I lookin' at?"

"That ain't piss," she replied, and he heard a bit—just a *bit*—of fear in her voice. "I don't know *what* the fuck that stuff is, but it ain't piss."

"Call Duran. Call it in." Anderson's heart was pounding. He felt some fear himself, but it was overshadowed by excitement. Something was happening here, by God. Something insane that had fallen right into his lap. This was more than a chance to boost his career; this was a chance to go *nationwide*.

He tried to step forward and felt Diaz's hand on his shoulder. "What are you doing? You're not gonna go *in* there?"

"Call Duran," he repeated, and pulled out of her grip. His hand went to his belt and drew his service pistol. Behind him, he heard Diaz dial into her radio, but he didn't allow himself to focus on what she was saying. All of his attention fell on the kid's bedroom. It was everything the Carr girl had described: a slimy, viscous den of horror. He even saw the dead lizard, right where Eileen had said it would be. *The late Jazz Carr*, he thought, and suppressed a mad giggle.

But it was the bathroom, he knew, where he would find the real prize. *C'mon, Connie boy. Show me that big beautiful head of yours.* Anderson knew this would be disgusting, but all fear of puking had abandoned his mind. He'd happily barf his own brains out if it meant getting to be the one to break this case. Anderson saw himself giving interviews to the press, describing in grim, somber tones how he'd been the first to discover the kid's mutated, warped corpse. He'd make Homicide within the year! Shit, within a *month*!

His hand found the doorknob to the bathroom. In the living room behind him, Diaz was talking to the dispatcher, describing the scene they'd walked in to find. Anderson twisted the knob and pulled.

The thing must have heard him walking through the room, must have been coiled and ready on the other side, because the door was not even fully open before Anderson's vision was filled with something huge and pink and wriggling, like a giant ball of earthworms that wrapped around his head and sent his entire body crashing backwards to the floor. He never had a chance to scream; his mouth was muffled by some awful, slimy appendage ramming its way down his throat.

It was a fucking *tentacle*, he realized in a blaze of panic. One of many. The rest coiled over his face and upper body like a tangle of pythons, pinning his arms and squeezing the sides of his head so tightly, Anderson felt his eyes were about to pop from their sockets. Somewhere, dimly, he heard something that might have been Diaz screaming. It was hard to hear anything over the wet, sick writhing that had engulfed his entire world.

Something shifted in the pink fleshy mass that pinned him. The tentacles gave way to a thick, knotted mass of squiggly grey tissue. The mass was divided vertically down the middle, two distinct hemispheres covered in wrinkled fissures, the bottoms of which sprouted out into the octopodian tentacles now holding him down.

The average volume of an adult male brain is about 1,300 centimeters. The creature currently strangling Officer Tim Anderson had grown to more than three times that size. The rest of Conrad Carr's body had died in the bathroom, but his brain was very much alive. It pulsed with strength—and hunger.

Anderson was choking, trying and failing to scream around the bulk swelling in his throat. He had dropped his gun when the creature had latched on to his face, and it had splashed somewhere in the puddle of gunk covering the floor. Even if he had been able to reach it, his hands were bound tight, smaller tentacles weaving in between his flailing fingers. His mind was shrieking a single word—*DIAZ*—over and over again. Pinned as he was to the floor, Anderson had no way of knowing that his fellow officer had already fled the scene screaming. Wild horses could not have dragged her back.

Something was happening to the brain-thing towering over him. Flesh was splitting, dividing. From somewhere within the soft, fleshy mass there arose a sharpness, the tissue calcifying, growing hard and jagged. A lamprey-like mouth yawned open, sucking greedily, studded with tiny hooked fangs made to slice… and clamp… and drain.

If there was any mercy on Tim Anderson's end, it was that he felt very little pain as the thing's newborn jaws settled over his scalp. He was barely conscious of its teeth shearing through his skull to find the soft meat beneath. He felt only a great *tugging* sensation, heard the horrible sounds of suction and slurping, and then his terrified eyes rolled up white, and he ceased to feel anything at all.

The thing that had once been Conrad Carr gorged itself to satisfaction. It could feel itself growing larger again, Anderson's grey matter dissolving and redistributing within it. His nerve and glial cells joined its own ever-expanding collective; they rejoiced to meet their brethren.

The creature shuddered with ecstasy. This was only the beginning. Every new harvest expanded its intelligence, its perspective. Already Anderson's thoughts and memories were being digested and repurposed, new synapses forming, new pathways opening up. With more minds, more meals, there was no limit to what it could do. What it could *become*.

But there was no hurry. It intended to savor Anderson. It would not stop until every last scrap of neural tissue had been licked clean from the man's skull. *After all,* the creature thought happily, *a mind is a terrible thing to waste.*

MEAT OF THE STARFISH
JOE KOCH

On Feast Days, when they clean the cages, Misha roams the great yard as the servants scrub, wishing only to re-enter that ecstatic darkness that follows excision in the comfort of his gilt and padded prison. He bitches about the hot sun to one of the husbands.

The older, heavy-set man indulges him. As a favorite pet in the Aqilodin's collection, Misha exploits his privilege with careless cruelty, cultivating infidelity without risk of execution. He wouldn't even bother talking to the man if he'd remembered to bring his guitar outside today or hadn't gone so long without relief. Two whole weeks.

Misha's meat has been harvested for months in preparation for the Aqilodin's quaternal feast. She stages the erotic displays between his bouts of regeneration. At the last event, after marinating him in her mouth, teasing out Misha's engorged blood, and nearly gnawing through his corpus cavernosum raw, the Aqilodin handed the boy the cleaver to make the final cut himself.

The thrill among those gathered was palpable. The Aqilodin's audiences vie to return and eat the meat of eternal life at her pleasure. They fear being banned from immortality by her capricious rage. The hush and sweat-damp pressure of a crowd hungry for his gift makes Misha feel like a god, mangled and erect at the center of their excitement.

It's always been like this.

He hovers on the brink of an abyss in these moments before the Aqilodin or one of her select completes his pseudo-slaughter, the murder of his cock. His regenerative member has been handled, hacked, and harvested by all of them at least once before today in what the Aqilodin breezily calls artisanal preparation.

On that last occasion, Misha briefly imagined what he could do with the cleaver, imagined slamming it down on her skull to split her face in half the same way he imagines his cock splitting her groin and breaking her detestable body apart when she requires his service. He'd swing the cleaver around the room to undo every grinning, panting visage, paint the walls with flesh that will never regenerate, for Misha alone has this gift that enslaves him, excites him, infuriates him, and since he's never known any other kind of love, he brought the cleaver down in one decisive, orgasmic self-amputation.

The immediate rush of unconsciousness was, as always, glorious.

Now the banquet is nearly ready to begin.

"Look," Misha says, unlacing the drawstring on his pants, tempting the older husband to fondle the Aqilodin's property and risk a death sentence for it. Heft and grizzled edges are attractive to Misha, far more appealing than the uncanny youth of their shared mistress's wiry frame and chemically plumped ass and mouth.

He pulls it out, proud of its size, impatient to erase it in another grotesque orgy. "See? It's wet at the tip already, long and solid after two fucking weeks."

The smitten man gapes as the shouts of protestors beyond the electrified gates warn that the guests are returning. Misha seeks privacy in the shade in response, though he can't say why he bothers. It's not his problem if the old man gets caught.

The husband behaves strangely. He isn't rough. One hand caresses Misha's brow and chin instead of his exceptional cock. Misha doesn't know where to look with someone gazing into his eyes. It gives him a warm, almost sick feeling in his stomach.

Chants of dissent carry across the grounds as the usual rebellion at the gates grows louder. Yet the man's gentle hand refuses to rush.

"Light of the night sky," he murmurs in earnest. Misha pushes him down. The man understands. He dips the huge head in and out of his lips between more sticky words. "Tiamat… show me… her lodestar, your sign… guide me."

"Shut up," Misha says.

The commotion and chanting escalate. The Aqilodin's militia is taking too long to quell the outsiders. Annoyed, Misha pushes harder, arching his back. The man takes him deeper—yes, tongue cupping the underside, Misha swelling against the pressure of his soft palate—but then pulls him out.

He looks up at Misha, reverent and childlike. "I will swallow the ocean you offer. Show me your signal. Let me follow."

Gunfire pops like fireworks at a distance. The commotion at the gate grows louder.

"Sure. Hurry, before you get yourself killed."

Sadly, the husband says, "The bitch has told you nothing. The sacred heresy, the theft. I wish there were more time. Mark me now. Pour your light into my willing mouth."

Taking Misha all the way into his throat, the man sucks as if he no longer needs to breathe. More gunshots ricochet over the growing uproar of disintegrating chants, of screams and cheers. Engulfed, Misha rams his heat harder, seeking that exit into delirium he craves. He can't find it in the slack maw of the old fool who tenderly shields his teeth, pressing his lips into the shaft with protective care.

Misha thrusts faster, rougher, upsetting the man's tempo, grazing a chipped tooth. The streak of pain ignites him, almost banishing the sick, warm feeling in his stomach. Whistling sounds, smells of something burning, as if slamming into the old man's jaw kindled live fire. Misha pictures himself as a rock scraping aged flint. The head of his cock could crack open to spew lava. How bad it would hurt. The tiny lips in his glans would burn as liquid flame erupted, goring his whole length from tip to hard root, searing his hungry organ into a scar from the inside out.

He shoots into the man's throat once, twice, and then yanks out to splatter the drooling face with a thick white deluge, pumping into the air and stumbling back as hot shining arcs slather his target. Bullseye. A real bullet whizzes by, and then another. "Oh, shit."

The next one hits.

Feet trample the manicured grounds. Voices in disarray, more running and yelling, smoke rising in the air. Misha milks the last aching drops from his yearning cock as the husband shudders from the bullet's impact. Stubborn supplicant, shoulders upright, neck stretched, his mouth hangs open to Misha's cum. A black and pink chasm.

White dollops on the quivering tongue. Bleeding from the chest, the husband grapples at mixed fluids, stroking his torso as if he could swim inside his own body to escape drowning.

Glistening white liquid smears into milky red as his soaked frame heaves, fails, and collapses.

Mouthing something unheard, his lips are pasted with pearls. Misha hits the ground beside him in the chaos of fire and smoke, confused by tears that spring unbidden, unreasonable, with no connection to any emotion Misha can name as the corpse gives up trying to speak.

The sun darkens, though moments ago it was noon. Clouds press downward. The sky turns the color of a storm, or an eclipse.

The Aqilodin's palace is in flames.

Staff and husbands flee or join the violence. Guests lie dead. Wounded militia, rounded up, kneel at gunpoint among the rare lilies and vines around the fountain. Activists have seized their weapons and set the Aqilodin's collection free. A white tiger prowls toward the open gate. Three enormous exotic birds perch on the Aqilodin's statue at the center of the fountain. Water still pours from its two stone-carved breasts below a youthful, idealized face. The brightly-feathered birds preen, oblivious to the hostages and shouting dissidents.

A cheer resounds. Gathering in tumultuous procession, the multitude hoots and jeers at the Aqilodin as she stumbles, dragged between two muscled women who wrench her arms forward at the head of their vengeful parade.

Blood smears her nose and chin. Her jewels are gone, robes torn open, wigs discarded to expose her balding head. She bellows in murderous outrage as the crowd takes turns pummeling, spitting, and tearing away the last shreds of her clothing and hair.

Misha wants to run to her, but can't. He can't believe what's happening, doesn't know if he wants to defend her or attack.

As the Aqilodin sags, begs, offers everything she owns as if it weren't already burning down, the rebels laugh and execute her surviving guards. She's forced down among the bodies and rare lilies, head bowed over a wooden bench at the seat of the fountain. Her icon looms above, adorned with indifferent birds.

A boy of Misha's age is led to the Aqilodin and handed an axe. He swings clumsily. Misha gasps. The axe lands in her left shoulder, just grazing the neck. She screams. People clap. The boy struggles to yank out the weapon. In a gush of blood, he succeeds, and swings again.

This time he takes out a chunk of her neck. The partially severed head wails like a tortured cat. The body writhes. The crowd cheers. Her murder is nothing like Misha had imagined. Even at this distance, it's loud and more grossly intimate than sex. The axe comes down five more times before the juddering atrocity of her is split and silenced.

In celebration, the crowd tosses the Aqilodin's head like some sport. Misha stays hidden, holding the dead husband's hand. He doesn't remember grabbing it and can't seem to let go.

Then, less than a meter away, the head crashes through the branches. Before Misha can react to the deflated thing, the mouth that ate all the meat of him, that meat now changed into the cells of a headless corpse—this thing with its eye sockets like runny eggs; broken teeth—how he'd liked to have broken them himself, fed them to her. Except, maybe not—lolling tongue like a deformed elastic, an elongated slug, concave cheeks. Before he can run, or grab it, or throw up, celebrants burst through the shrubbery to fetch it.

They halt. Smiling, they tell Misha to be calm, as if placating an animal. Someone approaches with the Aqilodin's keys, unlocks his collar, and hurls it away. A muscular woman holds the Aqilodin's head up in front of Misha as he huddles beside the dead husband. "You're free, little starfish! See? You can go back to your people now."

A victory song sweeps the rebels away.

Ash drifts as the palace is consumed. How quickly Misha's home vanishes. His toys and golden cage, his music and guitar are all gone. The meat he supplied to the feast is charred, lost in the wreckage. The celebrants dance long into the night as the colossal bonfire dissipates into darkness, finally trailing off in groups and pairs as cold descends over the embers.

The dead husband's hand is clammy. Strangely heavy. Like clay, it keeps the imprint of Misha's fingers where he has clutched all night. The body teems with flies, ants, and some other emerald-colored insects. Misha rolls away and stands to piss.

The tiger has wandered back onto the grounds. Lazily, it tears at one of the guards slain among the lilies beneath the fountain. Water still flows from the stone-carved breasts of the Aqilodin's statue, but the birds are gone. Misha wonders if the tiger will eat her body, thus eating him. He finds a detached comfort in the idea, or maybe it's more like rage.

He creeps from the bushes to find her. Brown, plentiful birds peck at mounds of colorful plumage on the ground, pulling away long red shreds of exotic meat with sharp, hooked beaks. As Misha edges closer, they flap and screech, alerting the tiger, who sniffs the air.

Misha backs away.

Thirsty, hungry, sickened by the cloying sweet rot, the spent smoke and decay, Misha doesn't know where to go. He spends hours avoiding the open gate.

He can hardly believe he was once curious about the outside. An early memory returns as he looks across the threshold, a blue-toned day in summer, trying to sneak away on Feast Day. The alarm in his collar squealing as he dashed behind a supply truck piled with lemons. The sharp citrus tang blasted by exhaust; the shouts of men, their overwhelming arms.

A thrashing would have been better than the coddling he received from the Aqilodin. He should be grateful to be kept safe from poverty and the dangers of the raging sea on the coast. He was so special to her. She'd nursed him as her own. Misha bit his tongue until he swallowed blood as she kissed and petted him in her lap. He could only end her cooing by compliance, grudgingly reciting, "I love you, too."

"That wasn't so hard, was it?" Her chemical breath receded as she lifted him down from her bony thighs, handing him off to a guard. He spent another of many nights unable to cry or fight, unable to feel anything but numb, burrowed into the soft velvet cushions behind his cage's gold-plated bars.

Still numb now that he's free. Reminiscent of captivity, he has nothing left to lose. Has anything really changed? When he dares the winding road outside, something eases in his chest. He breathes a little differently. The older husband's shoes are too large, but better than going barefoot on sharp gravel. He went back to the body for them, and also took a ring with an inlaid pattern of lapis and a smooth, turquoise-colored stone. The colors drew Misha's eye. He'd never seen anything quite like it. A curving five pointed star design that gave the impression of swirling motion as the pattern caught the light, as if the central star swam across a cerulean sky.

His fingers are too small to wear it without falling off. It stays cool in his pocket through the afternoon heat, a man's ring, large and heavy, a pleasant balm. Touching it makes Misha feel connected, though to what, he couldn't say.

By sunset, he arrives at clearings, fields. Old cars, a cow or goat here and there, claptrap structures Misha doesn't recognize as homes. He spots people going in and out of the buildings, chairs on porches, potted flowers, fences. Many doors and posts are ornamented with a swirling star painted in colors similar to the dead man's ring. Others made of metal achieve a turquoise tone by verdigris. Misha wants to ask the people what it means, and if they really live in these small huts. He wants to ask them to feed him, to pamper him with admiration, to tell him where he can find a new guitar.

Anyone who might have answers averts their gaze. As Misha passes the farmsteads, every inhabitant avoids him. He steps through a lax open gate. A woman singing a cheerful melody drops her wet laundry at the sight of him and ducks indoors. He doesn't think to steal a shirt, even though his bare shoulders and chest tingle. He's never been outdoors this long, never had a sunburn.

Later, he imagines sucking the liquid out of the wet laundry, twisting the fabric into a tight cylinder to nurse his dry-bloated tongue. Intoxicated by the thought, he throws his head back and pitches forward with eyes closed. The road has long since given way to dirt, much softer on his feet. Hunger like a drunken ache as he reels—music, voices. Ahead, a large building with a partially open front. People gather, standing or dancing in groups or pairs. Inside, tables laden with plates of food and communal jugs.

Misha's baffled by the way the servants speak to the diners. They chat and laugh with a brash familiarity that would have warranted censure or death in the Aqilodin's service, and yet, like the farmers, they ignore him as if he's not even there. He finds a chair at a small table near the kitchen. It's stacked with empty cups and plates. No one brings him food or water. Diners murmur or point and turn away. Misha stands up and positions himself to intercept the next tray that comes out of the kitchen. As he plucks at the sleeve of a lad bearing a jug brimming with gold-colored liquid, a tall woman stomps out from behind the bar, clapping her hands, snapping a cloth at Misha, and yelling, "Shoo, shoo, shoo!"

She drives him away from the diners, away from the music and camaraderie of the patio, back to the road. Misha doubles back, sneaking through the weeds. He circles the exterior of the building, captivated by the smells from the kitchen. In the back, dogs prowl and eat from a small heap where a bearded man in an apron has hurled scraps from a bucket. He scans the backyard briefly, expectantly, and then goes through a Dutch door that he leaves open on top.

Heat wafts out. Misha crawls closer. He can't compete with the dogs, frightened by their snarling rivalry, revolted by their matted coats. The shadows they cast look like monsters. They stink, and the sickening trash smell mixes with savory kitchen fragrances and damp dog. The ache in Misha's stomach ingests pain and rot, disgust and desperation, trying to feed. Instead, his gut ferments dizzily until he dry heaves.

When he looks up from the weeds, the man with the bucket is at the door, peering suspiciously out into the dark. Misha holds as still as he can on his hands and knees. Strings of his saliva trail down. Soon, the man leaves.

Much later, the building grows quiet and nearly dark. The dogs run off, chasing some small prey invisible to Misha. The heap has depleted into a shallow pit. Keeping an eye on the door, Misha ekes forward and digs out bones to suck, some wilted vegetation. Miraculously, he uncovers an untainted clump of roasted, spiced meat with seasoned carrots. He hunkers down, stuffing his mouth with dirty fingers.

He doesn't hear the Dutch door swing open.

Doesn't notice the bearded man in the apron until he lights a pipe.

The smoke is different from the tobacco or hash at the Aqilodin's palace. Peculiarly watery and herbal, it's a thick fragrance with a touch of bitterness. The man's eyes wander the distance beyond Misha, who swallows hard and stays down.

The man speaks loudly, orating across the empty yard. "They say that before the power plant emblazoned the night sky to light up the playgrounds of the rich, our people had a special relationship with the sea." He draws from his pipe and takes a few meandering steps. "Our grandparents fished, swam, dived, found medicine there, and taught a way of being that moved with an ocean's wisdom, a tide's elasticity."

Pacing, he's aimless, yet somehow closer to Misha. Low in the trampled weeds, in the dark, Misha hopes he blends in with the pile of dog-eaten leftovers.

"They say things were better then. At this time of year, a certain type of star conceived from the confluence of the two firmaments would plummet down like a fallen angel, blazing, and land at the vanishing point where the sea meets the sky. A strong swimmer could reach that line of oblivion on the horizon and capture it, the key to eternal life. The sacrament was only allowed to our kings. In those days, there were only good kings. They didn't rule, but served. For anyone else, the meat of the star is heresy."

Almost directly above Misha, he drags on the pipe several times and exhales at length. He lowers his voice.

"When I flew into the horizon as a young man, it matched my pace ever farther, the line of oblivion endlessly receding. You see, our grandparents were stronger than us. And there are no more kings."

He grabs Misha by the hair and hauls him inside, squirming and yelping.

"Wash," the man says, releasing Misha next to a large water trough with a primitive tap. "Then rest." He points to a cot crammed against the wall. Beside it, a stool is piled with fruit, bread, roasted corn, bowls of freshly stewed meat. The room is oddly angled and barely big enough to turn around fully without knocking something over. "Eat all you want, little starfish. I'll be back tomorrow night."

When the door locks, Misha kicks it, doing more damage to his toes than the wood. His feet have been sliding around in the too-large boots all day, blistering. He curls down on the floor, hugging his stubbed toe. The singular, focused pain of it unlocks a trembling in Misha's gullet that rattles him deep into his core. His chest constricts, his throat catches, and he does something he hasn't done for more years than he can remember. He cries.

The man in the apron returns as promised, long after dark, after the clamor of diners has come and gone. Misha's smelled the fragrances of many dishes cooking, eaten a good portion of the food provided, and washed his body and filthy pants, taking care to keep the ring from disappearing down the drain. He hums along with the music outside as long as it lasts, lying on his back, hands fretting in the air as if his guitar wasn't reduced to ash. Some part of him warns he should be afraid of being locked away in this place, but a cage is a cage.

When the door opens, Misha follows the man as beckoned.

"Do you think I could get a guitar?"

The man smiles. Still wearing his apron, he's tall, full-bodied, with cascading dark hair and a full beard. His movements are slow, but not indolent. Heavy and certain, he leads Misha into the cooled kitchen.

He holds Misha's slender shoulders. His breath is full of herbal smoke and a clash of many flavors tested during his work tonight.

"My brother once served under your mistress, may Tiamat curse her rotting corpse. He told me how you were stolen from the sea and made a feast for heretics. You have a chance to start a new life here."

"Okay."

"Listen," he says, arms encircling Misha, pressing his ear to his chest. Misha sinks into the soft flesh, feels its warm rise and fall. The rush of an urgent heartbeat is interrupted by erratic gaps. "I'm not afraid of paying for my sins in the afterlife, but I want—I require—more time. You shouldn't be here, but what do I have to lose?"

He releases Misha, who isn't sure he wants to be released. The warm and almost sick feeling in his stomach has come back, the feeling from his encounter with the older husband, although this time it's more of an ache. Misha asks, "Where is the sea?"

The man shakes his head. "Far, far to the east, beyond the sunrise. Clogged with garbage and disease. One can't go back to the past, only forward." His hands go beneath his apron. "May I see it?"

Misha's chin rises. "Get on your knees."

How he misses feeling like a god, misses the majestic descent into darkness, the days of blacking out. Three strokes and his cock stands up as if it were an arm reaching out to grasp the man, who, having obeyed, leans forward, mouth first.

"You've tasted my food. You know my skills. I will only hurt you in ways you desire."

Misha invades his throat violently, nearly gags him, and then stops.

"Do you promise to cut it off?"

"Yes, oh yes," the man says, catching his breath. "I will make the most exquisite dish. That bitch never prepared the meat of eternal life in the way it was meant to be done. You feel it in your loins, don't you, in your love for other men? The power of your gift?"

He's risen, and standing now, so much taller than Misha, arms strong from years of butchering, lips wet with saliva and pre-cum. Misha's caught by a sudden impulse to run, a flash of distrust.

The man bends, reaching down to scratch his knee, and then he's behind Misha, over him, tying his wrists and ankles. He hoists him, trussed like a goose, hooking the rope on a huge metal pot rack that spans the wall. The bolts hardly rattle as Misha struggles. His cock wobbles, comically half-erect between forcibly bent knees.

"Hey, this is dumb! I—I like you, okay?"

Lighting a burner, the man places a flat cast iron skillet on the flame. "The meat must be marinated from the inside out," he explains like a patient teacher. "Lesser chefs fail to understand. The tough outer layer of muscle is thin, yes, but very unpleasant to the teeth. Like chewing rubber. It must be seared crisp, nearly burnt, yet no carbonization should be allowed to mar the delicate oceanic flavor of the spongy tissues within. This cannot be accomplished with a harvested member. The meat must remain naturally engorged throughout the process of searing each section so that the center stays moist."

He tests the skillet with a drop of water. It sizzles into smoke.

"You're not going to die," he tells Misha, approaching to fondle what he will devour. "I need you erect, and I need you alive. You have to stay awake. This will be a test of your endurance, but I have faith in you, little starfish, and herbs will keep you alert. You may grow, over time, to enjoy the process, as you've learned to enjoy other agonies. Try."

The man bends to suck and stroke. It's impossible for Misha to will himself flaccid, impossible because the terror at being burned alive that pumps his veins into thrashing whips beneath his skin is wired straight into his cock, wired into his desire, his imagination, his conditioned response, and can he hope with this inclination to find ecstasy in anything other than greater and greater excess, in more glorious brushes with death? Isn't he nothing but his gift, nothing but his cock, a thing to be milked and butchered—perhaps one day for good, perhaps this time will be the last, his cock dragging him with into darkness in a final torture orgy of death—and shouldn't he be happy with that?

In his best imperious voice, he says, "Turn around. I want to marinate it in your ass."

"Ah, that will create a very special flavor. The enzymatic reaction—"

"Shut up. Bend over."

The chef obliges, working his way onto the shaft with a handful of spit and hard backward thrusts. Misha writhes. The rope shifts. One hand comes free behind his back.

He leans into the grasping fist of the tight sphincter, into the sound of the man's moaning. His broad buttocks, the hint of fur on his back, the sheer size of him impaled and vulnerable arouses something more complicated than hatred. If only the man had talked it over with Misha first. If only he'd asked.

But he didn't. Misha works at the rope until his hands and feet slip free.

He holds onto the rack, and then in one great forward thrust, he pushes off from the wall, stabs his cock deep into the man's guts, and shoves him headfirst into the stove top.

Moans shift into shrieks. His long hair catches fire. The skillet clatters, or maybe the man's skull breaks, or his nose or knee shatters. Misha doesn't wait around to analyze the crackling and splintering sounds or shoot his load in sadistic triumph, doesn't want to, feels strangely sick and guilty—why must love always be like this? He runs all night, runs and stumbles until his feet shred on gravel, keeps stumbling forward until he's back inside the perimeter of the Aqilodin's electrified gate.

The white tiger lies wheezing on its side in a pool of vomit among the lilies. The colorful birds are mere traces of scattered plumage and tiny bone. Misha fails at fitting the ring back onto the corpse's bloated finger. He stores it in his pocket for later and finishes undressing the corpse.

Once he's undone the drawstring on his own pants, Misha picks up the sharp-edged chunk of gravel that he's chosen from the road and makes the first cut at the base of his cock in a quick slash.

For a split second, there's no blood, no discomfort, only a pristine mental silence, and then suddenly—fire. He gasps. Red beads stream down each side of his cock. A burning sensation blooms within, like pissing gasoline. Misha breathes through the pain, determined to stay conscious, to make good on his word, even if his promise to the husband came in a moment of thoughtless cruelty.

The next two cuts he makes are longer, slower, more agonizing as the stone edge scrapes with blunt imprecision from each corner of the first gash to the tip of his glans. Misha grasps the peeled skin, prying the wound open. He yanks, yells, and stops, freezing with pain, ready to give up, ready to vomit. Forces himself to breathe, and yanks again.

The pain begs him to black out.

Half blind with hot tears, he persists, proving himself, choosing who gets his gift, placing the bloody flayed strip of his living meat on the husband's cold skin.

Cutting, crying, and peeling again, stripping his regenerative member, divesting his groin of all flesh, Misha wraps the dead husband's body. He stretches the mangled tissues thin, tacking them together with sticky blood, smearing some trace of connective tissue across every gap.

When he's cut away the last of his cock, sliced it down to nothing and completely swaddled the corpse, he collapses and allows his consciousness to fade. The blackout comes not in a glorious climax, but in soft rolling waves.

When Misha wakes, the husband stands outside the gate, squinting at the sunrise. Misha notes the position of the mountains relative to that direction, studies for a moment how the shadows fall. He slips the ring back onto the man's finger and takes his hand. It feels good, large and warm against his palm, cupping his thumb. They walk.

THE DAUGHTER

On the eve of your first expedition, your mother comes in the night to braid sweetgrass and baby teeth into your hair. Your birthday party was earlier this evening, so your belly is full of aerosol frosting and cornmeal cake, your limbs are heavy from running around in the courtyard playing Blind Man's Pit until your cousin skinned her knee and ruined all the fun. You went to bed so tired you could hardly manage the trek up the rickety stairs to the washroom. Even now, your limbs hum with the pleasant ache of excess, but you wake up anyway.

There is no moonlight in this part of town—the Body blocks the moon from sight entirely—and it takes your eyes a long while to adjust to the dark. You don't recall feeling the mattress dip when she sat down, and for a second, you're trapped in the treacle-sticky dread of not knowing what exactly woke you up, before you decide it doesn't matter and the dread slides off your back like water on vinyl. Your mother's fingers are in your hair, gentle and searching as she sneaks a strand free, then another. When she's done she rises and makes a sign with her hands over your bed, lifts the sackcloth off the night light and is gone again, spectral with worry.

You lie there for some time, rolling the tooth-beads between thumb and forefinger, knowing she would've tried to stop you from signing up if she could. But only under-thirteens need parental permission to join the mining teams, and you went to the company office first thing when you woke up this morning. When your mother saw you with your hand on the doorknob, she didn't say a word.

#

Your first day on the job begins with rubber. When you turn up five minutes late because of traffic in the high street, the foreman hands you a pair of waxy coveralls, their folds so heavy you have to lean against the wall to distribute the weight.

"Bit big on you," he says as you pull them up over your clothes, "but you'll grow into them."

Next is footwear. Not a lot of folks can afford the special grippy shoes, but there are some treads you can strap onto your regular ones. In the locker room, you can't stop staring at the miners' kit, jangling with charms and little pouches of ash and spice; whatever keeps the spirit of the Body from following you home at the end of the day and peeping in your windows.

"I don't believe in spirits," you tell the foreman, but he takes one look at the sweetgrass and teeth braided into your hair and laughs.

The miners in the locker room don't look anything like you pictured them—broad shouldered and thick bearded, mid-forties, same age as your Pa when you saw him last—and men like that *are* here, sure enough, but most fall unsettling far from this age range, either too young or too old. You recognize one of the girls from down the block, and you're sure she can't be older than nine. When you catch her eye, she looks away quickly.

After the coveralls and the shoes, there's hard hats and grappling hooks and giant foldable bags made of grainy plastic, which one of the older women tells you to hook onto your tool belt.

"That's where the meat goes," she says around a mouthful of chewing tobacco. "You pack it in tight, and when you run out of room you turn your hat inside-out, use it as an extra bag." She doesn't smile with her mouth, but her eyes are bright. "Trust me. They pay by the weight."

The work bell rings and everybody files out, past the surly woman at the door checking punch-cards. Normally, it's each worker's responsibility to get themselves to the site on time, the foreman explains, but as it's your first day on the job, you haven't been assigned a site yet. He lets you come with him in the company tram car, a peeling husk of metal you've watched grind its way about Enfield for as long as you can remember.

You stand at the back, holding onto the empty window frame and watching smoke billow from the chute at the top of the car; it leaves long trails behind you. The tram clanks up high street; past the train station where they send the meat off to the city; past the shop where Morgan's mum sells expedition equipment to miners; past the shop across the street where Thomas helps his father launder the miners' clothes; past the market swollen with meat both holy and unholy; past the estuary where the waters are red, past town hall with the faded banner which reads *YOUR PAST IS MECHANIC, YOUR FUTURE IS ORGANIC*, and finally, you come to a stop beside the gaggle of tents surrounding the base of the Body, where mystics and shamans and fry-cooks hawk their wares.

"Decent curry, that one," says the foreman, pointing out a tent with yellow bunting, but you can barely hear him over all the yelling.

Here, you transfer to the cable car that draws you up, up, up the mountains made by the curves and contours of Body. Being so high up instills in you some sort of frozen dread, and the rocking of the carriage makes you queasy, but you can't help but lean over the side to get a better look at it: not the Body, whose shadow you have lived in all your life, but Enfield itself, your little town, so small and ramshackle, getting smaller and smaller, melting away as you slide up into the heavens.

"They're anchored into bone," the foreman says close to your ear, thinking you must be looking not at the town but at the cabins barnacled to the sides of the Body.

"We drill into the muscle, run rivets through 'em, hook 'em on that way."

The cabins, you'll learn later, are way stations and checkpoints for miners refilling water canteens, exchanging equipment, and loading up meat to be shipped off. Most of them are barely larger than the cable car, though some of the bigger ones look like two cabins cobbled haphazardly together and, on occasion, connected by dizzying railed walkways of sheet metal and clapboard.

You don't dismount until you reach the topmost knob of the Body's spine, arched in its insouciance, and this time when you look down Enfield is a cluster of specks, half-submerged in wispy clouds and smog. It's windy up here, like on a mountaintop; with no trees or rocks to take shelter behind or grab for purchase, you feel like a crumb in a strong breeze, buffeted about by the weather. The foreman shows you how to clip your belt onto one of the cables that traverse the Body's back, and pull yourself along until you reach the central station nestled in the dip of its shoulder blades.

There's a cantina up here, but the light inside is dingy and the three cramped tables empty. The menu hanging above the luncheon counter boasts a pickle and hard cheese sandwich that's double the price of the ones sold back in Old Town. The foreman pushes you gently toward the register with a guiding hand on your back, and the wizened man behind the counter peers over the till at you, squinting, before shuffling out of sight. After a moment, he reappears and hands you a card that was clearly once laminated, but whose plasticine edges have long since frayed and curled up.

"Site 493." The foreman peers over your shoulder. "That's the western flank, entry point between the third and second rib." He straightens, scratching beneath his cap. "Lucky kid, that means you might get to see the heart."

#

Inside the Body, it is very dark and very wet.

You've had rudimentary schooling on mammalian anatomy, seen the diagrams of the naked man—always a man—with his skin peeled back to reveal first the musculature, then the nervous system, the internal organs, and at last, the skeleton. You always pictured the inside of the Body—and all bodies, generally—as red, but now you're learning that isn't always the case. There is red here, to be sure, but there's also yellow and blue and brown and other colors, sometimes. The fat is yellowy and easy to cut through, and comes away in revolting lumps. The veins run blue and purple through this place, and one of the miners tells you candidly that it would be wise to learn which veins are which, in case you get lost.

"Find the right artery, no problem, you just follow it 'til you come to an organ and you'll know where you're at. Right as rain."

You know it cannot be that simple. Your father knew the Body like his own, had its pathways memorized the way a supplicant knows a canticle, and the knowledge had not saved him. You don't say this to your new coworker.

Instead, you ask, "How often do people get lost?" knowing full well it's an average of three a year, and that none of them has ever come back.

You're walking through a tunnel carved into the muscle. It's dim here, and suffocatingly claustrophobic. Up ahead, your new coworker ponders your question, a gloved hand running over his wiry mustache.

"Dunno about official numbers, but I'd say one every six months? It's a big place, lots of ways to go astray."

"But how—" you can't help yourself, "How's that possible? There's no way to walk off the path, right?" There are no roads through this place that weren't carved by human design. Animals won't touch the Body, won't eat of its flesh. Parasites won't burrow into it. Birds leave it untouched. Everyone knows the only creatures that eat the Body are humans.

The man up ahead doesn't stop to look at you, so you keep walking. Your foot slides on something slick, but the woman behind you helps you keep your balance with a firm hand at your elbow.

"The stats are in your favor, miss. Some thousand, two thousand workers a day out here, and only one gone missing every half-year? You got worse odds someplace else, surely."

This figure does not account for explained deaths, you learn the next week, when a way station on the north side of the Body falls away, dropping the five men inside three thousand feet onto a slab of barren thigh on the shelf below. You aren't there to witness it, but swear that when it happened, you knew. Heard the thud of meat on meat.

"Must've over-excavated the area where the station was anchored," your friend Marta says without sadness.

"Lost some structural integrity. Happens sometimes. Not for a while, though," she adds, catching your eye. "Not all that often."

The incident doesn't make the papers.

THE GRANDFATHER

Your father was a farmer, as was his father before him. Most of the men in these parts were farmers, and you too were a farmer until the Body came.

No one saw it appear. The place that became Enfield was quiet and sparsely populated, a place where, aside from circle dancing on Wednesdays, everybody was in bed an hour after sundown. It came at night; tremors in the earth as it laid down to die. Your wife woke you, pulled you out of bed, and the two of you huddled under the doorway waiting for the quake to subside.

78 miles long, 32 miles wide at its base. Hundreds of acres of farmland gone in the blink of an eye. *Imagine that*, you say to your daughter, who is born on the day the Enfield mining company rolls into the countryside to nurture the seed of industry. *Imagine waking up one day and finding a mountain at your doorstep.*

Your daughter is older now than you were when the mining began, with a daughter of her own. When Clem was small, she asked a lot of questions. *What did the Body look like? Why did you decide to become a miner? Did you have horses? Was Mr. Enfield very handsome?* You answer these questions (it had more skin on it back then, everybody who stayed became a miner, we had horses on the farm but sold them to the company for pickaxes, he was average-looking) with patience and honesty. You used to fancy yourself a teller of tall tales, but there are no tall tales anymore. In the shadow of the Body there is only truth.

"People were very frightened," you tell the child. She sits on your knee sucking rock candy. The kitchen smells like pipe smoke and tallow, and it's getting late, but your daughter isn't home yet. "Nobody knew what the Body was in those days. We were just starting out."

It had taken only a week to figure out that the thing did not rot. The holy flesh did not decompose, nor break down. No decay, no gradual dissolving of meat into itself, no collapse, no fester. Whatever this thing was, it was staying right here, and the town of Enfield would grow around it.

"This was a busy place in the first days," you tell her. "They brought in scientists from the universities in the city, all wearing white, great suitcases of instruments with them, all shiny. None of us had any idea what they were doing, scrambling the way they did. Stayed for a few months, some as long as a year, and then they left scratching their heads. Enfield had already arrived by then, and things were getting crowded."

Clem sits up, taking the rock candy out of her mouth and holding it up to the bare bulb overhead, watching the light shine through the amber. "Did you ever see a vision?"

You shake your head. "I never saw anything in there I couldn't explain. It's just meat and bone, girlie. Nothing to worry about."

"Lex said her brother saw a vision when he went in," she presses. "He saw—" she scrunches her face up; the act of pinning down the story requires great concentration. "He saw a light that said words to him, only he couldn't tell what the words were."

"It happens to people," you say, because it does. "But not to me."

You've heard that in the city, they gather in parlors and drawing rooms to eat the holy flesh, to see the light and speak to it. Not here, though. What devouring happens here occurs behind closed doors, or inside the Body itself.

"I did hear a voice once," you tell her, because she must be appeased and because it's true. "My first week on the job, I got lost. I thought I heard someone calling to me. Sometimes it sounded male, sometimes female, sometimes like my crew mates."

Clem's eyes are very wide. The piece of rock candy lies in her open palm, abandoned.

"Were you scared?"

"I was very scared. So I took my pickaxe and I chose a direction and I cut, which is very dangerous, but of course we didn't know that in those days." You mime the swing of a tool. "And I chopped my way to the surface."

"Don't tell her things like that. I asked you not to tell her things like that."

You both look up. Your daughter stands in the threshold, empty basket at her hip and a sour look on her face. Her hands are raw from scrubbing.

"She asked. Do you expect me to lie?"

Your daughter sets down the basket and crosses to the sink to refill her thermos. "Tell her you won't talk about it."

Clem slides off your lap and runs up to her mother, thrusting the sticky lump of candy in her face, squawking about something that happened at school that day. You take this opportunity to rise from your chair and move to the front room, moving the curtains aside and opening the window to ash your pipe onto the street below.

From here, you can see the tiny pinpricks of light—red, warm yellow, bright white—blinking from stations along the Body's eastern flank, and the ones way up along the spine which are often mistaken for far-off stars.

THE MOTHER

There's a custom in Enfield to take the bone of an animal with you into the mines, and to bury another bone from the same animal in your garden or nearby your house. The bones are drawn to each other, and thus it is said that you will always come home.

Your husband carried the wishbone from a chicken around his neck, but that wasn't enough for you, so one morning you go to the yard and pull one of the dog's canines out. The dog, an elderly mutt with a shiny black coat, doesn't know what's happening until after it's all over, and you see the way it looks up at you with its big eyes, mournful and confused yet still trusting, and you suppress the urge to vomit. The tooth becomes a pendant, another trinket-weapon in your arsenal of godliness. When the dog dies a year later, you make sure to hide the rest of her teeth around the house: tucked away beneath floorboards, under pillows, buried in the window planters. None of it helps, in the end.

The day he goes missing is very ordinary. Looking back, it's the normality that really galls you, sets your nerves on a knife's edge, gets your temper up. It's a Monday, and it's sunny out; you can see blue in the sky when the breeze lifts the smog.

You're at the laundry until late, watching the basin run red from the miners' shirts and trousers. Sometimes you think you should have been a miner. Your hands are strong enough. In the evening, as the sun is slipping beneath the ridge of the Body's shoulders, you return home. Your husband isn't here yet, but that's not unusual. You don't begin to worry until long hours have ticked by. The stroke of midnight passes, but even then you tell yourself he's fine. You leave the kitchen light on and go to bed.

This was before your father's injury, when he was still a miner; in the days and weeks that follow, you will question him again and again about the last time he saw your husband. They left together in the morning, as they always did, walked to the base camp, rode the cable cars up. Assigned to different work sites, they parted ways and never met again.

"I was site 92, large intestine," your father explains over and over, "he was sent out to site 720. Brain stem."

When the shift ended, he'd waited for your husband at the base of the Body. After an hour passed, he'd assumed they'd missed each other by accident, that the other man was already at home, having supper without him.

You are not paid the widow's stipend because your husband cannot be officially declared dead. Instead, you're gifted fifty credits to spend at the company store, courtesy of the foreman. The flour it buys lasts nearly two months. When you remember those long days, you can still taste fried dough on your tongue.

When you discovered you were pregnant with Clementine, your husband brought you a gift wrapped in waxy butcher paper. A slice of the placenta, he told you.

He had never been assigned to work near the womb, but knew a guy who had. Your husband watched you eat it, and when you finished, you smiled at him with coppery blood in your teeth.

Clem has scarcely worked in the mines for a year when her grandfather dies. It takes you and Clem a week to scrounge up the money for a burial, and in that time you discover that your father's body refuses to decompose. This is convenient but unsettling. In the end, you cremate him and erect a headstone in the churchyard, where your husband's body will never lie, where your husband's tomb will never stand.

And all this in the shadow of the Body.

The Body is a massive, sucking thing. It pulls in people and repels animals. Not even the bugs and worms and maggots will gnaw at its flesh. According to your father, the arrival of the Body altered the weather itself, its huge mass changing the patterns of air flow and pressure. The Body confounds you. Sometimes you visit it, tearless, and the two of you watch each other with a kind of understanding that is a lack of understanding. A mutual agreement not to understand. It, like that dreaded day, the worst day of your life and every other day since, is ordinary. Its meat is holy, but it is also just meat.

THE DAUGHTER

Bodies, you have learned, are mostly water. Being inside a body (or Body) involves a lot of sloshing and squelching. Here you are, knee-deep in gore from a tunnel collapse just north of the kidneys, wading through rich fluids. You've got to keep your gas mask on in here, you're so deep in the tissue.

You lean on the wall beside you. It caves slightly under your weight, pink flesh reforming to accommodate your hand. Liquid wells up between the fingers of your glove. Beside you, the company man makes a noise of disgust, muffled beneath his mask.

"Let me guess—" You smile at him despite yourself. "Shareholders didn't quite tell you what you were signing up for?"

"I'm from the university," he replies, offended. "We have *administrators*, not shareholders."

You shrug without respect. You're sixteen now, an age perfectly suited to disrespectful shrugging. "The company owns the university, so."

You let the point make itself, turning back to the path. This area is, as far as you know, mostly unexplored and largely unexcavated. The main sites are clustered around the largest muscles—gluteus maximus, hamstrings, femoral quadriceps, lower back, pecs—and the meat coating the organs tends to be tougher, deeper, more dangerous to navigate. In here, at the very center of things, you're acutely aware of how close you are to the underside of the lungs—which, when accidentally punctured, run the risk of releasing carbon dioxide into the Body's many highways and cavities. Puncturing the stomach, too, can be dangerous. You've seen your fair share of bile-burn wounds, and you've no desire to experience one yourself.

Today's assignment has proven taxing. The surveyor keeps stopping to make notes on his waterproof clipboard, capture photocard slides, examine tiny wobbling creatures under the lens of his portable microscope. According to Marta, nobody has sent a surveyor in a long time. They write papers about the Body, but don't need to actually see it in real life to write the papers: the gory trek through the arteries and tracts lost its glamorous appeal way back in your grandfather's time. Whatever this guy's after, he's not gonna return home with bragging rights, that's for sure.

"Why did you come here?" you asked him earlier that morning, but he just blinked at you and said "For the

Body, of course," as if you're fucking stupid, and that was that. No more friendly chatter.

When you first started this job, you were plagued by nightmares where the Body comes back to life with everyone still inside it: muscles begin to move again, blood begins to pump. Tendons spring to life, flesh tightens, the whole mountain of meat contracting, grinding like the gears of a great clock. You grew out of the nightmares, but traveling in this deep reawakens an old sense of choking anxiety. Like you're racing against a clock whose face you can't see.

"Did you know this meat is holy on a cellular level?" the surveyor asks amiably, stopping to collect a sample of cells from the cavern wall. "It's true—we've watched it up close. Not even microbes will eat it." He pauses. "They're what causes decomposition in regular food."

"I know what microbes are." You readjust your head-lamp and then, out of pure knee-jerk urge to fill the silence, you ask, "You think they're still here?"

"Still here?"

"All the folks gone missing," you hear yourself say, before you can think better of it. "Could they—I mean, they couldn't survive here. Not for very long, right?"

You expect the surveyor to laugh, but instead he scratches his chin.

"I'm not sure. They might. There's water in this place, plenty of it and reliable ways of harvesting and filtering the moisture. No worry about disease or bacteria, though you'd develop deficiencies in a number of vitamins, especially vitamin D…" He trails off and begins again. "It's possible that humans could sustain themselves on this meat, even though an animal wouldn't dare."

"You sound pretty sure." You can feel your boots sinking gradually into the mire. You need to get moving soon, or you'll be sucked in.

"We've run trials," the surveyor says airily, preoccupied with the swab-sample he's depositing into a slim plexiglass vial that hangs by a cord from his neck. When he moves, it clacks noisily against the ID card suspended from his lanyard.

"At the university?"

"What?" He looks up as if you've roused him from a dream. "Oh, yes—we arranged for some rats and pigs to live off the stuff alone, total darkness. No access to any resources but the meat, of course."

"What happened?"

He smiles grimly. "They ate each other instead."

You get the go-ahead nod to begin walking again, and the two of you continue down the tunnel. Its circumference is too narrow in places, and every once in a while you're forced to go at it with your hacksaw.

"Of course," he goes on, "animals cannot reason, so they cannot simply *decide* to eat of the Body, the way you or I might. They have only their natural instincts to rely on. We'll be starting human trials soon."

"And people sign up for those, do they?" You try not to laugh.

Another smile, and he meets your eyes and tells you the plainest truth you've heard in years. "People will sign up for shit you would not believe."

"Yeah," you say at last, turning away. You're moving forward, sliding up to your thighs in reddish sludge. Someone ought to drain this area soon. "That's true."

Yesterday you got to visit the cavernous excavated space around the femoral socket, totally stripped of tendon and sinew, the arch of the pelvis held up by steel beams so many hundreds of feet above your head, and when you saw it, you were struck for the first time in three years with the realization that some day there won't be a Body anymore. You try to picture the skeleton where once a mountain stood, all gaps and negative space, the rib cage casting stripes of shadow across the land below. And eventually, even that will be gone, picked over by scavengers, sold for scrap materials and scrimshaw. The Body does not decompose in the traditional way, true, but what is decomposition but a process of redistribution? You think of the Body now, chopped into cold cuts that can be found in every butcher shop and grocer in the nation. You have not seen the cities, but you know the meat is there, flashing pink and white from the windows. Sometimes when you close your eyes, all you see is the slippery gleam of wet meat in the gathering dark, and you know that it's eating you back.

Your science boy—that's how you've come to think of him over the last few hours, though he's surely twice your age—wants to collect samples from the womb, so that's where you take him. You entered the Body this morning through a porthole cut into the flat steppe of the lower back. From where you are now, it's another hour to the pelvis proper.

Gravity works in strange ways here. Or perhaps, more precisely, it's strange that gravity should work here at all. In a place like this, you ought to be floating weightlessly. Even three years in, the pull and tug of your own weight still catches you unawares: how easy it is to plunge through a membrane or put your foot in an unstable pocket of fat. If not for your grappling hook and sharp-eyed friends, you could have drowned on more than one occasion.

When you reach the womb, it is not what you pictured. The area around its northern side has been cleared of muscle and debris, the intestines crowding one end and a bit of space at the other. Organs have been moved around and sectioned off to accommodate a small work station. You have always imagined wombs as vaulted, hollow, and full of light, like the diagram of the cathedral in your history textbook, but this region of the Body is as ill-lit and claustrophobic as any other.

"We're taking amniotic fluid today," says your scientist, kneeling to unbuckle the canvas-clad object strapped to his back. The cloth falls away, revealing a metal tube, a bit like the ones they use to extract ice cores, equipped with what looks like some sort of plunger mechanism.

A couple of miners are already present on-site. A foreman and your science boy are engaged in a heated debate of some kind, interrupted occasionally by lab coats asking clarifying questions about pressure and tension and metric tons. The miners sit on the sidelines, leaning against an outcropping of stray bone, avoiding each other's eyes.

#

There is no alarm bell this time. There is no warning. If there were red flags, you don't have time to look back and identify them.

When the flood hits you, it knocks all the air from your chest. Your head pounds. Spinning on an axis, finally weightless like you wanted in the gush of womb-water that rips out of the tear in the lining where the puncture process went wrong.

When you wake up on a stretcher at the base camp three days later, you will be informed that the accident killed seventy-eight people, including three foremen and five lab coats, and that everything south of the rib cage is, in effect, underwater. You should be dead, but so should lots of people who are still breathing, so you don't worry about it too much. Your mum is hysterical, talking about packing up and moving someplace else, but you both know that isn't an option.

"I saw Pa in there," you tell her, and for the first time in your life she gives you a look like she's thinking about wringing your neck.

"I saw him," you tell her, "when the womb burst. I saw him."

She asks you not to talk about it ever again, so you don't. In June, you return to the mines. They assign you to work on the westernmost flank, on the opposite side from Enfield. When you stand on the ridge of the spine and use your binoculars, you can see a smattering of shanty towns bubbling up around the western base. Soon there will be more Enfields. You think about asking for the surveyor's name, the one who drowned in the mines that day, but you never do. Wondering where his grave is, what his obituary sounded like.

You've started avoiding mirrors. Your friends are happy when you return to work. Marta is especially relieved; she actually cries when she sees you, wraps you in a crushing hug, even buys you an overpriced cantina lunch to celebrate your reinstatement. They were pulling corpses out of the mines for a solid week after the flood, she tells you, teary-eyed, over her food. One of them looked just like you, and she thought you were dead until she heard you'd been rescued and rushed to the clinic. Must have been some other girl, poor soul.

You ride the cable cars every day; the view still takes your breath away. You like to stand at the Body's highest point to feel the cold wind wrap its arms around you. The air up here is so crisp, absent of ash and smog and soot. Most days, you are so, *so happy* to be alive. Sometimes you catch your reflection when you're doing the dishes, but all you're able to make out is the slippery gleam of wet meat.

SOUTH COULEE SINKHOLE

MARY SANCHE

[Pictured is a photograph of
a Richardson's ground
squirrel taken from a low
angle, as though the
photographer is laying
down flat. The squirrel is
yellow, fat, and has large,
glossy black eyes that
reflect the mid-morning
sky. It is perched on the
edge of a hole of light
brown dirt about the
diameter of a vinyl record.
A silver sagebrush plant is
out of focus in the background.]

Wow!! This must be the biggest ground squirrel burrow I've ever seen! Delighted to have captured this sight in the hills this morning. Biologists, sound off in the comments—do you think this one has a big family? Or are they just an over achiever? [Heart eyes emoji.] [Hole emoji.]

#wildlifephotography
#wildlife
#wildlifephotographer
#animalphotographer
#wildlifepictures
#wildlifelovers
#natureperfection
#natureisbeautiful
#natureinspired #ourplanet
#wildlifeperfection
#wildlife_conservation
#canada #canadianwildlife
#alberta #albertabadlands
#canadianbadlands #prairie #grassland
#richardsonsgroundsquirrel
#gopher #nikon #cute #rodentlove

\#

Jenny checked the comments on her photography account. Her squirrel shot had been up for about ten hours now, and it was performing about as well as she had expected: wonderfully average. @jen_has_a_camera had a modest following, but she was proud of it anyway. It made hope slosh around in the back of her head. Someone might pay her for her photo work, one day. She just had to keep cranking out content. Grinding that grind.

There were more comments on the ground squirrel than she'd anticipated, and many of them lanced her with sweet hits of dopamine.

angiee_yyc_
Wow, great shot!

land_n_skye
Cuuuute!!

daniijavez
aww i love him

Others were standard Alberta crap and trolls.

angel_xx_mom

I shoot these on my farm. Vermin

jcjohnsson398

Ewww why would you take a picture of a gopher

eff_one_50

Hit one of those with my truck today, popped like a balloon

oilbud2020

is that a rat? gross

What she was really hoping to find, though, were the ones from experts. The researchers and other wildlife photographers that followed her feed showed up further down as she scrolled.

ab.wildlife.foreverr

I've never seen one make a hole that big either. Did it enter the hole? Were there tunnels branching off from the bottom? Wonder if it might be made by something else… American badger?? Old coyote den? Any sign of erosion around the edges? Cute shot nevertheless! Look at those big eyes [Heart eyes emoji.]

badlands_backyard

Is the hole still under construction? Looking forward to seeing progress shots lol

meera.biologist

I did my master's study on abnormal burrowing behavior in mammals. Will DM you the link!

magnapaulina

Wowwww get this squirrel an award & a cold beer

Jenny checked her DM　s for the link to that paper, downloaded the .pdf, and promised herself that she would read it later.

#

Sweat squiggled down the back of Jenny's legs. Spring had crisped into summer, and the badlands ate up the heat and yawned it right back to her. South Coulee was generally five to ten degrees Celsius warmer than the nearest city at this time of year, too far from the cooling kiss of the Canadian Rockies. The muddy river that snaked between the hills was only good for hatching insects. It wasn't her first rodeo, though—not by far. Born here, raised here, Jenny was used to the dry, roasted summers.

She had her bucket hat, long sleeves, hiking shoes, water bottle, and camera bag. Her Nikon was trained on a mule fawn sleeping in the shade of twiggy aspens. Fawns were gold for her photography feed, bringing in likes, comments, and views like birdseed brought sparrows. They were sweethearts with their spots and doe eyes, and the camera loved them. Jen loved them, too.

The mother deer stood guard not far away, head bent to native grasses, ears alert. Jenny kept her distance. The fawn was bedded down against yellow-green, the shadows from branches double-dappling its speckled hide. Behind it, overgrown with wild rye, lay the remnants of a mining cart, a century-old relic of the valley's coal boom.

She was sure she'd sweat through the sunscreen on her calves, but the wait was worth it: the fawn raised its sleepy head, blinking dolly lashes. It looked right at the camera. Jen's teeth could have rotted out of her skull.

Her shutter snapped in quick succession. The quiver-beat of bees' wings.

Gravel snapped beneath the toe of her boot.

The fawn was up and running, spidery legs thrown out in youthful panic. Its mother was already well ahead, bounding cleanly through the parched scrub and up the flaking side of the hill.

Too new for such blinding grace, the fawn scrabbled along the bottom of the coulee. Jenny's lens followed, shutter speed cranked up to freeze fleeing limbs and flagging tails.

Suddenly the fawn was down again. Out of frame. Tripped. It had pitched forward, nose in the dirt, forelimbs buckled, lost behind the sage bushes.

Jen lowered her camera and straightened up. The sweat on the back of her legs was like ice. If the fawn had fled because of her, and hurt itself somehow—

As she made hurried strides toward it, the baby unfolded upward, found its footing, and shot off up the hill after mom.

Jenny exhaled. The sun beat down on her as she made the rest of the way to where the animal had fallen, sidestepping prickly pear cacti and scarlet mallow. There were barely any hoof prints in the hard-baked earth, except where they scraped gouges in the edge of a hole.

The hole.

The one from her photos.

It had gotten bigger.

#

On her next day off, Jenny went back.

She had spent her last few shifts thinking about the hole. Ringing up groceries was not her true calling, but it paid the bills, and between scanning barcodes and weighing produce, the hole persisted. She thought about the ground squirrel perched on the rim, and felt less certain that the animal had been there out of ownership. Maybe it had been curious. Looking in, like she planned to do. *Needed* to do. Maybe it had been going about its ground squirrel life, innocuous, and the hole had tugged it closer, like the fawn. Like herself.

Now, Jenny pushed forward through the stagnant heat of the coulee. It was like opening the oven door. She tugged the brim of her bucket hat low over her face, a ward against the sun.

The hole, now larger than the mouth of a municipal garbage bin, exuded a faint sickly-sweet smell. It was not an unpleasant scent, but it was different the usual bouquet of the badlands. Amid the aromas of ripe sage leaves, sun-baked ironstone, and the pungency of invasive weeds, the hole's perfume served as an anchor. It sat in the centre, low, deep, and earthy. The faint tang of salt.

Tide pools came to Jenny's mind. Lazy deltas with sullen, dark seaweed. Dead things in shells. The promise of decay—but promise only. The sort of smell that she knew would get worse.

The rational part of her brain provided an answer. Maybe the burrow belonged to something larger. A mid-sized carnivore. Something with a meat-sweet diet. A heavy, animal musk.

Slipping her Nikon out of its bag, Jenny levelled the lens at the hole. Snapped a few photos. Swapped out her lens. Snapped a few more.

#

[A photograph of a burrow
against the hot summer
background of the Canadian
badlands. A single red
dragonfly is suspended over it
in sharp detail. Dry grass in
yellow ochre bends over the
foreground, out of focus. The
hole is as wide as a coffee
table, dwarfing the dragonfly.
Swipe to see the same natural
feature with a lens cap for scale.]

@jen_has_a_camera
Hole update! This burrow,
which I have photographed
before, keeps getting bigger.
Did you know that the stone
in this area of Alberta is soft?
Erosion can happen quickly
in a world made of sandstone,
mudstone, and bentonite.
However, it hasn't rained
recently! [Shocked face
emoji.] I wonder if someone

new has moved into this
burrow… What do you
think? Red fox, coyote, American badger??

#natureperfection
#natureisbeautiful
#natureinspired #ourplanet
#wildlifeperfection #canada
#alberta #albertabadlands
#canadianbadlands #prairie
#grassland #holeupdate

#

The next time Jen visited the hole, it was worse. A strident tang of stomach contents screamed at her nose. Flies hummed in the depths. A few rose like lazy smoke, blood-drunk and heavy. She waited for a swell of wind to temper the miasma before she stepped forward, hoping to see what poor animal had tripped, gotten trapped, expired—but the hole was brimming with flies. The reflex to hold her breath was strong, persistent; she sipped air through her teeth to spare her nostrils.

She swallowed down her curiosity and turned away before the wind died down.

A dead deer festered in her mind's eye. Large enough to stink that bad. Hot and bloated in the sun   .

Before an enterprising fox tore it open at the belly, maybe, wetting the parched earth with bile and acid; Before keen crows dipped down into the hole to have their taste of deflated deer eye.

Good for the crows, she thought. Good for the flies. Nature had to eat.

Except she hadn't seen crows. Hadn't seen a fox, or coyote. Only the flies had been there, and the smell wouldn't leave her nose for days to come.

#

A barrier had been erected around the hole. It was half-assed, already failing: orange mesh strung up on rebar offcuts, drooping on one side. Jen could see the perimeter of the hole already creeping past the extent of a plain square of plywood. A brittle, sun-damaged pylon sat atop the plywood, bearing the remains of a spray-painted Town of South Coulee acronym. A sign flapped in the hot breathy wind, held to the mesh by an inadequate number of zip-ties. "DANGER: SINKHOLE" had been written on it in black permanent marker.

Town of South Coulee, hard at work, Jen thought.

As if this introduction of garbage into the natural environment would do any good. As if it would keep anyone out. All she had to do was stomp the mesh down and lift the plywood out of the way. If she really wanted into the hole, she'd be in it.

The thought of lowering herself down into its fusty depths was not new. She had thought of it before, while checking the hits on her photographs, or in the break room at work. Jen was no stranger to curiosity and this instinct only seemed a natural progression. She would have made a fine biologist, keen on field work, if she had not done her degree in photography instead. She was sure the hole had to contain answers. Answers that Jenny doubted unfinished plywood could contain.

She posted her next #holeupdate with a photo of the garish plastic mesh, and a sly jab at the Town's perfunctory work.

#

Jenny turned off the vibration on her phone. It had begun to buzz happily in her back pocket, the likes and comments rolling in. A reshare account had picked up her series, recapping newcomers with a cheeky influencer who asked, wild-eyed, "What's in the hole?"

Comment after comment echoed them. *What's in the hole?*

Badger was the leading vote so far, but Jenny had her doubts.

Even still, a badger settled in her mind next to the previous tenant, the dead deer. The badger ate the rotting meat. Mustelid snarl drooling black slop. Fur bristled down its back. Paws as big as bears, meaty hands growing. Something wrong eating something just as wrong. Jenny had the utmost respect for nature and its brutal cycles, but this hole, it was something beyond—

"Excuse me?" The customer checking out at her till snapped Jenny back to Earth.

She looked down at her hand. A ripe nectarine, half squeezed to death on the stainless steel scale. Her thumb boring down into the fruit. Juice flickering in the red streak of the barcode laser.

"Oh my God, I'm so sorry. I'll go get you another one from produce—"

"No, that's alright. I'll just take the other two."

Wiping her sticky palms on her apron, Jenny sweated through the rest of the transaction. Treated the two surviving fruit like precious eggs. Carried on with her day. All through the rote succession of beeps, keystrokes, loyalty cards, and counting change, though, the badger scrabbled at the back of her mind.

#

Summer heat dogged the long dark hours of night. Crickets sawed persistently. Jenny listened through the window screen, unable to sleep. She held her phone above her face, a dim rectangle against the dimmer murk of her apartment's ceiling.

Jenny had pulled up the scientific paper sent to her by @meera.biologist, titled *Strange Renovations: Atypical burrowing behaviors observed in small mammals of the midwestern United States of America.* It wasn't Canada, but some of the ecosystems would be comparable to her local area. Animals didn't care about the human construct of borders.

The abstract explained that the data had been collected by numerous field teams as a collaborative effort, and the lengthy list of co-authors—Dr. Meera Falk-Mahmud among them—reflected that. Through the analysis of burrows, the authors would suggest several factors contributed to the making of atypical burrows: internal and external traumas, human interference, and "other indeterminate factors."

The point of the paper, of course, was not to prove anything. It was to present findings— findings that consumed Jenny into the early hours, until the breeze through her window had cooled by a scant two degrees, and the crickets had ceased their pleading. Whether she read about prairie dogs, marmots, voles, or foxes, a pattern presented itself through the meticulously laid out research: animals had good hygiene. They kept their burrows clean, atypical or otherwise. Those that didn't were usually ill.

There were plenty of figures to back it up: photographs of bug-eyed beasts squatting in their own feces, the geometry of their dug holes upended and pointless.

Whatever was in Jenny's hole in the hills was sick.

\#

[Posted in a story format, which will disappear in twenty-four hours, is a selfie. Jenny, brown hair wild in the dry heat, luminous with flyaways, wears a headlamp on a blue elastic headband and a gray-and-pink 3M respirator. Her DSLR camera hangs from a strap at her neck. She gives the phone a gloved thumbs-up.]

\#holeupdate
I'm going in!! Wish me luck!

\#

Even the orange mesh had fallen. What metal posts still remained leaned over the hole, resigned to their fate; The rest dangled on tattered plastic halfway down. The plywood square was gone—she assumed she would find it at the bottom when she got there. Jenny tied a nylon rope to an immovable granite erratic and draped it into the blackness.

It wasn't as deep as she feared.

Eight feet down, her hiking boots met plywood with a damp thunk. The air was humid, sighing like a sleeping dog, and as Jenny swept her headlamp around the perimeter of a hole, she found that it diverged into a tunnel.

Above her, the hot blue sky was a flat disc. The blazing sun was impotent. It should have reached that eight feet to the plywood, but it didn't. The hole swallowed up light.

Tiny insects jostled for space in front of her headlamp and eyes.

She was glad the respirator kept out the smell.

"Okay," she breathed, raising her phone, and started recording. The mask wrapped her voice in plastic. "There's about two and a half feet above me here. It isn't that deep. There's a tunnel on this side that branches off. I'm going to go slow, see if I can get some pictures."

She posted the video to her story. Comments rose like the flies, urging her to be careful, asking her if she was qualified, fretting about the badger that Jenny had stopped suspecting. She swiped them all away. Her nose hitched up at their concern, bunching against the respirator. Over the years, she'd been told that she didn't have the heart for *real* art. Didn't have the hunger, the determination. All she had was a mid-rate photo feed and a safe job at the grocery store. Well—fuck them. She *did* have the guts for it. How many insect bites had she endured for the perfect shot? How long had she crouched in the grass, knees in the mud, lens trained on a moose until it lifted its crowned head?

This hole was her proof. Her daring. She was down here, and she was going to get her fucking pictures.

Crouching, Jen snapped a shot of the receding tunnel, its opening set in a synthetic highlight from her headlamp. Flies hovered in front of her like ghosts. The soles of her boots scuffed against the sandy plywood, leaving it behind. Heading in.

Her crouch turned into a crawl. When her creeping palms found fur instead of earth, she froze. The chorus of fat flies crescendoed, flushed from their feast of deer meat by her coming. It *was* deer—hollow, coarse hair in tawny summer brown that came free and stuck to her damp hands with the barest touch—but it wasn't the shape of deer anymore. It had been stretched. Flattened. Once a deer, now it lined the circumference of the tunnel, desecrated and plush.

Jen pressed the respirator hard to her face, reinforcing the seal. Beneath it, her upper lip was drenched with sweat.

She scrambled back. The thought of leaving—returning to her nylon rope while she knew she could, calling the town, the RCMP, was there—but Christ, what would they even *do*? More orange mesh, more pylons. More neglect.

And she still needed her photos.

Jen squirmed until her ass was on the floor, raising her camera between her buckled knees. *Click,* with flash. Flies like occult orbs floating in the foreground. The background: deer-hide, deer gut, darkness.

She swept her plaid sleeve over her brow. Replaced the lens cap. Crawled forward.

Something still sighed hot air from deeper in the tunnel. The fetid breeze tickled the raised hairs on her forearms. Nothing in this ecosystem breathed that loud—not even the cougars who came down from the mountains to claim territory of forgotten barns—but even with that dread swelling in her stomach, Jenny couldn't help but move forward. A taut string from her sternum to the centre of the world tugged at her, they way it had tugged at the deconstructed deer. The way it tugged each fat fly around her head.

Fur gave way to offal. It was impossible for Jenny to find purchase on serpentine slicks of small intestine strewn in irreverent heaps. A slight downward incline was all it took to send her slipping, falling onto her shoulder with a solid wet thump. She coasted head-first down blood and clay, gasping curses into her respirator, trying to right herself, all while feeling sticky butterflies in her stomach. She was getting closer.

But to what?

Coming to a sludgy stop at the bottom of the incline, Jenny rolled back to her hands and knees. She patted her pockets for her phone and couldn't find it, but her camera was alright. *Thank God.* She cleared the muck from her headlamp and passed the beam over her new surroundings, tracing the paths of heavy wooden beams, black with age. Some had fallen, constricting the tunnel to half its width and height.

The hole had sucked her into an old mine.

Jen's insides tightened. Even in their heyday, these tunnels were dangerous, prone to collapsing. She did not want to be down here for very long yet something still plucked at the front of her mind. Consciousness wrapped around a claw. Animal instinct.

I'll be fast, she promised herself. Planted her knees. took a photograph, the flash popping back up from the body of the camera.

The viewscreen, slick with blood and clay, showed her streaks of the resulting photograph Timbers rose in stark contrast to the surrounding tunnel, flicking the flash back at her with their oiled grain. Posts and lintels, frames within frames, receding into the darkness where the couldn't reach.

It was a far cry from cutesy wildlife photography, but it felt *important.* She had to document this.

Jen let the camera dangle from its strap around her neck and crept forward, placing each foot carefully in the red-brown slurry. Transferred her weight downward even on her toes and heels. Low centre of gravity. No more slipping.

The tunnel was humid enough to keep the mud on her clothes from drying.

She should turn back.

This was dangerous.

People died this way.

She would die this way.

And for what? Her art? Yes. For her art.

One foot in front of the other. Boots caked with filth.

I'll be quick.

It had to be close. The tunnel split. Ahead, to the right, dead ends, earth slouching down onto ancient rails. To the left, more timbers, and—

There.

Hulking in a widened cavern replete with flies, there were bones. Sinew. Skin. Bigger than anything native to the surface landscape—bigger than the bison, even. Bulkier than a moose. It turned to face Jenny—*intruder*—with a head made from too many skulls a gaze comprised of too many eyes. The motion dislodged some of the eyeballs, which rolled down to splat wetly in the clay at its feet, trailing optic nerves like tails.

It was barely keeping its constituent parts together.

It wasn't finished yet.

Wasn't *complete*.

Shoulders caked in deer fur slouched as it shifted forward.

Jenny lurched backward. Slipped again. "Fuck!"

Head slamming back into the wet earth, her respirator slipped free, and all the putrid weight of the reeking tunnel came rushing at her, cracking open violent nausea and a splitting headache. Jen scrabbled to turn over before she vomited and added   her own animal mess to the rest.

The shambling beast twitched several necrotic noses. It smelled her; vinegar filth. Heard her cuss. It reached out a rotten paw, all wrong, and took a step nearer.

Jenny didn't know what it was, but it didn't matter. It could have been anything. A demon. An aberration. Hunger and the hunt made real. She didn't care. Her mouth was acid, and she didn't want her insides added to its dripping collection. She wanted to keep her guts, her heart, her lungs, her pictures, her integrity, her *humanity*.

Crawling backward, fast, she raised her camera.

Pressed the button.

Click. Flash.

Light blooming in the dark. Untethered eyeballs flashing back red, blue, reflective retina green, pupils shaking and spasming as the beast roared with unmade lungs and ragged throats. It had no eyelids to protect against the brightness.

Jen ran.

Each slip of her soles in the muck was only more forward momentum. Running, falling, catching herself. Her headlamp fell down around her neck bounced there, twisting spectral shadows of her own limbs in her peripheral vision, but there was only one way out: the same way she'd gotten in.

Jen could hear the thing bashing itself on the timbers behind her, already grown too large for its sinking lair, but more than that, she could *smell* it.

Cold sweat mixed with the clay and blood on her face. Her collar was soaked with bile.

Gritting her sour teeth, she turned to kick at the last of the mining framework. Mud flew from her boots in viscous clumps. The timbers shook. Groaned.

Somewhere down there, she had dropped her phone, screen still bright with comments warning her, worried, but there wasn't time. She had to go.

Back again. Back up. Flies in her mouth. Up her nose. Rising up the incline was a desperate scramble against gravity's greed, and more than once she landed on her camera, jabbing it into her sternum. *My fucking lens,* she thought, knowing it would be scratched all to Hell, but as long as the memory card made it—

As long as her *pictures* made it—

Fur, now. Deer. Coyote. Skins pinned up around the tunnel like a reverse esophagus, enough for Jen to find some feeble traction. Her lungs were stinging. Aspirated stomach contents. Bugs. Coughing. She ripped and tore as she went, dislodging, ruining, wanting to fill the fucking hole, trap that thing, make sure it never got out, never again, the Town sure as fuck wouldn't do anything about it, and—there was her rope. Her nylon rope. Dangling out of the dark.

Jenny grabbed it, wrapped it around her palms because her fingers were too wet to hold it securely. Squeezed the life out of her wrists, but it didn't matter. Up, up out of the hole, the stench of that thing growing, hearing it thrash and roar somewhere behind her where she couldn't look, but Jenny was coming out into the sun now.

The *sun,* and the coulee shifting. Heaving.

Jen scrambled over tumbling stones and bright, swirling dust.

The hole fell in on itself. Swallowed hard.

Granite erratics, dropped long ago by heedless glaciers, stoppered the entrance, the nylon rope twisted among them.

Jen collapsed into a bed of creeping juniper, rolling onto her back. Sucking deep breaths of sun-baked warmth, she smelled sage on the air, clean and medicinal.

She felt for her camera.

Still there.

The hole was gone, but she had her proof.

OLD NEW STOCK
REBECCA BENNETT

Mar once broke their arm in three places, a mistimed jump from a swing at its zenith, but it's been a long time since that sickly feeling has swooped across their stomach. The feeling of organs levitating, then crashing back down with the snap of a bone. Out of their body one moment, fully within the next.

There's that same shift of gravity displacing itself as Mar stares down at the stretched skin and two folds of their belly, where a hard-ridged VHS tape is slowly, steadily pressing itself further in. The skin on either side separating and sliding apart like molten cheese. Malleable and soft, Mar's belly button has widened into a gummy smile as the tape somehow works its way in. The instincts to fight, freeze, and flight all coalesce as the cassette, warmed and reeking of burnt dust, wedges itself into their body. Slipping past all resistance of skin, fat, and muscle.

This is happening. This is real, and it's happening at *work*, in a musty basement teeming with broken arcade machines, house spiders, and dust mites, with a poster of Tank Girl looming over Mar's shoulder, tongue waggling in solidarity. Mar can't pretend like when they pissed their pants lost in the woods, imagining the worst possible outcomes as nighttime set in, telling their parents it was just spilled water. The shame stayed longer than the stain.

The labelled side of the VHS still hangs partly outside the folds of Mar's stomach, the tip of it extruding to match Tank Girl. The skin around the area is already puckered and wrinkled from the years Mar has spent cycling through weight gain. The writing is upside down: *Felicity's Birthday 1993*. The text is a neat, flowing cursive; the green ink long-since faded and moldy. Mar has watched the tape since its static-ridden beginning—so far there's been one episode of *Star Trek: The Next Generation*, a ballet recital, and a dress up for first day of school—but no birthday. It looks like it's the same family across the recorded home videos. One of Cherie's thrift store finds, probably shoved between *Fox and the Hound* and *Forrest Gump*. F for fucked up. Which is stupid, because Mar has seen worse things: creepy uncles, parental fights, nursing home visits, and some deeply awkward *Everquest* LARPing.

Mar wiggles their fingers through the squeeze between the tape and their belly button and into their body. The VHS is there, gears churning as it winds itself tighter. It should be   impossible. But their finger skims pebbled plastic and moving parts. Hot and wet and somehow real. Mar's hand comes away bloody—they tell themselves it's no different from a leaky diva cup. No different, not at all.

The blood jolts them back into their body. A breathless plummet away from the memories, from the comparisons to past understandable pain. Mar yanks at the tape. Pulls, and pulls, and pulls. It slides out a little, a peek of once white gears now glistening pink. Mar grits their teeth and yanks a little harder, short and sharp. The cassette lid hinges open, but instead of shiny black tape, there's a fleshy casing that's wrapped itself around a spool. The more Mar pulls the tape, the more they feel the corresponding twist from inside.

That's *them* stuck into the tape, their body, their organs. *Intestines*. Gross word, gross   er to see it. It's an inside word, meant to be whispered across the dinner table. Not displayed in front of them, impossible to refute or ignore. Mar holds the body-warmed tape in their hand, debates about screaming for Cherie, or trying to wake themselves, when the VHS player at the TV clicks and whirs. The same sound when a tape is inserted.

The TV is on, grey static gaining volume as the pulsing in Mar's ears dies down.

Continuing to pull out their intestines seems like a bad idea, so Mar closes their eyes, and shoves the tape back into place between the folds. The gore is gone, tucked safely inside again. The TV glows in response, the machine almost purring as it lights up. Normally, Mar loves the whir of tape as it readies itself to unspool; the hurried pitch as it sometimes ejects itself for no reason, like it doesn't even want to be played.

The static warps and colourizes, shuffling through finer and finer filters until the screen holds on an image that Mar has seen before. It's the tape that Mar ejected, needed to hold to their chest and comfort. The one now lodged into Mar's body yet somehow playing itself.

The video starts with a girl. White with long golden hair—princess hair. Young, somewhere between the age of too-old-for-rattles but too-young-for-skateboards. The kitchen is faux-luxury; hand-sponged walls, mahogany cabinets, and orangey marble countertops. It should be overstimulating, but with the kitchen table in focus, everything else is just a brownish blur. The camera is held sloppily, the voice behind it laughing in that wild, high-pitched way only a child could.

"I told you, if you don't comb your hair, then you don't get to have any." The presumed mother stands behind the girl with princess hair, dragging red fingernails digging into the girl's scalp. There's a sneer on the woman's face but also a veil of delight. Maybe she feels powerful for once.

Mar's seen that look, felt that look.

The scissors snap open, divide the hair, and snip.

Mar imagines the soft fall as the clumps of hair hit the floor.

The kitchen is a cacophony of noise: percolator in the background, dog howling offscreen, a child still laughing behind the camera, the mother shearing in front of it. Only the girl is silent. If she moves, her head is tugged back into place. The hair is shortened until it's choppy and fluffy above the ears, a blunt bang crooked on the forehead.

It's a mushroom cut. Hideously rendered, but then Mar has also never seen a good mushroom cut. Dorothy Hamill has ruined so many childhoods. This is just another one for the pile.

This is where Mar paused the video. They felt a stress blister forming on their chin, burning through layers of dermis, hot and weighted. It happens when Mar lets themselves feel something, when they get stuck in a memory that clutches too tight. Their skin bubbles and rashes until Mar is a puffy red rectangle that everyone avoids.

It doesn't matter what button Mar presses on the machine. No amount of tapping Eject or desperately clicking the remote has any reaction. The tape is embedded, the player is working on its own.

Instead of the mother cooing at her daughter's bulbous hair, Mar hears something else.

"I don't get this, I'm fine with the—" There's a gesture in the pause, Mar doesn't need to look up to know it. The dismissive wave, the tilted chin. "But Martin is at least a family name. Mar isn't even a full name. It's a syllable. It's nothing."

"Thanks Mom."

Mar looks back at the screen—the kitchen is the same, but the people have changed. The camera is steady now, the room is heavy with silence. It's just two people, Mar and their   mother. Mom has curlers in her blonde hair, a gentle sprinkle of grey at the roots. She looks delicate and light, while Mar is weighed down from layers of arm socks, hoodies, and emo-teased hair.

"Oh, don't give me that, Marlene. You know what I mean. It's fine, I'm *fine*, but you're telling me calling yourself Martin is out of the question? Or something classic like Mark! And that's saying something—because I've known my fair share of terrible Marks. Your uncle, for instance. What does it matter if you're only using part of it anyway."

"Because that's not my name."

Mar would love a fast-forward button right about now. Whatever stress blister they felt with the hair chopping video, it's nothing to the itchy spread on their upper arms. If they close their eyes, the video stops. But open, it restarts.

They let the video progress in unintelligible, shuddery moments. Blinking hard enough to clear the memory from their mind. Each syllable becomes distorted and monstrous. It's worse—   because the moment still runs scripted through Mar's head. Now replaying it over and over instead of just watching it. If they watch it, let the tape run out, maybe it'll be over.

They force themselves to look at the screen where their mother is chopping up a grapefruit. Half on each plate. Everyday, Mar would leave for school with heartburn from the acidity, feeling their throat being eaten away. But it's the '90s, there's no such thing as too thin   .

Mom is arranging the fruit, mouth working quietly, so Mar knows the fight isn't over—   it's just been tabled. Face twisted in annoyance then brightening.

"Mar is not a name, it's a blemish." She says with finality. The dropped tone, the elongation of the 'a'. It's mocking in a way that Mar best understood from the locker room. An edge that tended to be accompanied by a cocked fist or kick to the shin.

The rest of breakfast plays out in silence, Mar dutifully cutting each segment of grapefruit. Their mother flicking through Good Housekeeping. Big sighs that Mar was meant to soothe sound tinny from the speaker.

Once the TV turns to static, Mar tries to eject the tape. Job done, thanks for the memories. Goodbye now. But it stays firm, not even budging far enough to see the gears.

Cherie flicks the lights to let Mar know the day is done. They don't talk beyond the requisite boss-to-employee greeting. Mar doesn't ask if Cherie knows she bought a demon tape. It seems like a rude question, considering Mar is paid very well for their not-a-real-job. Maybe demon tapes were part of the employment contract Cherie never got around to creating. Or, maybe, Cherie has a tape lodged within her, too, and this is the sorority bonding that Mar missed in college. That seems too personal, since Mar still hasn't gotten the nerve to ask what brand of fashion colours Cherie is using. Her turquoise hair hasn't faded and Mar is jealous. Besides, there's no heft to Cherie, she's all Pilates muscle and vegan abs. There's nowhere for a tape to be hidden.

No one sits next to Mar on the bus, not with the red splotches peppering their arms or the flares of blisters across their chin. The tape stays inside, still churning steadily even though there's no corresponding TV. Maybe everyone *except* Cherie has a tape inside them. An untold thing that people just don't talk about, like discharge or period shits. An appendix no one wants noticed.

There are no stories online. Nothing beyond boring college essays about *Videodrome* and ER stories of rectal insertion, and a couple really weird *Magic School Bus* fanfics. There's Gastroschisis, an opening in a baby's abdominal wall where the intestines exit through the belly button. Nothing about VHS tapes, though.

Mar wakes up the next morning tasting grapefruit. The skin around the tape is inflamed, bulging around their missing belly button. It's pinkish and firm, oddly-shaped as if their bowels have gotten jumbled about. Mar imagines it as a mess of spaghetti, noodles akimbo, splaying their way across Mar's midsection.

***

It's not the *feeling* of their intestines, pulled slowly through the gears of the VHS tape, that does it. It wasn't the spike of fear from yesterday as the tape slid between folds of flesh, as it   pulled at their stomach and worked its way further. Creating a steady internal yanking that radiated to the back of Mar's spine. A low-level ache like the one that comes a week before their period.

It's not pain, not exactly. It's familiar and foreign and insistent, but it doesn't *hurt*.

Mar has experienced worse in this basement. Their skin reacts so quickly, spots lasting for days, when it used to be hours. Something about the chill of the concrete and the scald of the computer tower's fan. It leaves Mar unsettled, mired between too hot and too cold.

The air smells like warm plastic and dirt, and it used to make Mar nervous, the sweet burning that emanated once the VHS player whirred to life. There'd be the iron-taste of static as Mar turned the TVs on and off, desperate for a little white noise to soften the day.

Cherie says this will all be an art piece one day; the tapes, the basement, unchanged since the '90s when Cherie was a teen. Every month, Mar's Mom calls to see if the place is still in business, asks when Mar will need to move back in. Like it's *expected*. Like she hates it and wants it at the same time, if only to tell Mar that they could have done more.

Somehow, it's worked out because Cherie only seems to fall upward. The space—part video rental store, part Instagram experience—with all its '90s kitsch décor (corduroy couches, colourful Dell computers made into displays, mountains of weighty TVs piled precariously on one another) is constantly booked as an event space. Cherie has the funds and the time to play at artistry, one of those rare millennials with money. She chased her bliss, and part of that was found footage. Mar works in the basement, booting the old iBook G4 and rummaging through boxes of recordable VHS tapes bought through auctions. The footage is digitized, labelled, and backed up.

A second hard copy is always made. Cherie prefers VHS copies, wants that grainy quality and imperfect sound. Wants the impermanence of the medium. Mar is paid well to sit alone in the ass-end of Cherie's Vintage, to press record and watch a home video in real-time. Digging through the archive, slicing out the keep-worthy moments that will play on a projector or across the pile of stocky TV sets. It's as much art as it is autopsy.

The TV turns on while Mar is staring at their stomach. Looking at the edges of the tape, wondering if it can be pushed out, how deep it rests.

Suddenly, *viscerally* remembering high school health classes and being told that everyone should only have an inch of fat on their body. Teenage Mar watching with sweaty dread as calipers were pulled out and everyone asked to line up for measurements. The memory of it is so sharp that it takes Mar's breath away.

The air changes when the TV settles into a scene, the hairs on Mar's arms stand up. Everything feels focused on the television.

The image sharpens on puppets.

Goddamn *puppets*.

It's Mar's health class, but now with stringed fuzzy puppets. Each holding up a caliper to measure around their tummies, the point of the caliper sinks into the felted skin and pulls out glitter when it approves. All the puppets get approval except the one in the back. The puppet wearing black and doodling on their sneakers. The teacher flails at the sky, arms spread and mouth agog. The whole screen shakes with disappointment.

Mar's stomach churns, stretching further as their bowels push against skin and wrap themselves along the outline of the tape. Cradling it like a baby. Nestling together, like Mar's insides want to read the demon tape a bedtime story.

A basketball player-puppet moves to the front of the line and faces the blackboard. It stretches its shoulder blades, arcing them to the ceiling like wings. There are no bones in a puppet—so a chicken wing, plucked and raw, superimposes itself over the felt. Flesh, fowl, and felt. The skin stretched so perfectly around the bones that the caliper couldn't even measure a pinch. Mar had wanted that, wanted someone to count the vertebrae of their spine. Wanted that look of approval from a classmate or stranger.

It's absurd. But probably less absurd than the way Mar can also taste chalk in the air, hear the laughter of the other teens, remember each facial twitch in the teacher's face as the calipers gripped more and more of Mar's body.

***

The tape is insistent.

Mar becomes acquainted with *Teddy Ruxbin*, *Popables*, and *Circus with the Stars*. The pile of VHS tapes keep growing and Mar keeps cataloguing them. Birthday (Surprise), Birthday (Happy), Birthday (Sad). There's no need to update their filing system for Tape

(Demon). No matter how many new cassettes Mar has shoved into their skin, the maw of their belly button won't part.

All the VHS players could be on, rolling through old reruns, and Mar's tape still finds a way to show itself. It's 35 years of trauma being replayed and there is no one to talk to about the demon tape that wants to torture them.

Mar sees their life through Nickelodeon; puppets and cartoons and painful teen acting. They watch classmates hiss the word 'lesbian' alongside a split screen of their Mom counting   carbs. Doubling the revulsion and disgust. They see themselves lost in the woods, pissing behind a pine tree, unable to hold it in any longer. The way it got everywhere and how they were found immediately after.

Mar's face stays flushed red, cysts breaking out across their cheeks. Upper arms almost numb under the spread of rashes. It's meant to be a 4-hour tape, but it just keeps showing new (old) memories. There's no bottom to this pit. Mar keeps waiting for the spikes to hit, for something to finally pierce and destroy them. But it all. Just. Keeps. Going.

Once the static cues at the end of the tape, Mar's bowels coil in sympathy, gripping the tape and tucking it further into the cavity of their abdomen. The cassette stuck inside them can no longer be traced. Mar has shoved their fingers in—worked through jammy and squishy textures—

but can't find the blunt edges of the tape. Even the protrusions are softening, only expanding and pushing against the skin when a particularly heinous musical episode of Mar's life replays. During the last one, when young Mar broke into a Coldplay a cappella and sang *Yellow* sadly at the audience. It's from junior prom, where Mar was on the sidelines not wanting to be looked at, while desperately, achingly wishing someone would.

Mar clicks Fast-Forward. Eject. Pause. Stop. Nothing.

There's one button, the red sheen of it catching in the basement light. Mar's intestines loosen and tighten, a bloating sickness that threatens to overwhelm. There's no release from the tape, it's burrowed where Mar cannot reach, and there's no hiding from the stories it wants to tell.

They hit Record.

MELODY IS HUNGRY
JESSICA DOUTSAS

Melody ogled the spread in front of her: a greasy burger piled high with toppings; golden french fries drenched in ketchup; crisp celery beside vibrant orange carrots; and a thick vanilla milkshake. Her stomach gurgled.

She reached for the burger and bit into the juicy patty, hoping for a fleeting second it would taste as good as it smelled.

A split second later, she felt something squirm on her tongue. Fighting back a shudder, she realized her mouth was now full of maggots.

Her date Brad—the hot football player who had never seemed to notice her until yesterday, when he cornered her by their lockers and asked her to dinner—was oblivious, to Melody's relief.

Melody typically didn't eat in front of people. At least not since she turned sixteen. After that day, anything that entered Melody's mouth rotted instantly. Meat became a slimy, decaying corpse. Bread blackened and crumbled into ash. Cheese turned to sludge, while milk soured and curdled. The rancid stench would make her gag, and it was impossible to stop the squishy mess of larvae and mold from escaping her lips alongside bitter tangy vomit whenever she ate.

Melody had been terrified at first, and tried to talk to her parents about it, but they said she was being ridiculous and refused to believe her. Eventually, she gave up arguing, and now somehow survived on the rotten nutrients she consumed.

Tonight, she naively hoped for something different. She wanted to be normal, to enjoy a meal, to impress her date. But as the maggots wriggled and the burger decayed, she knew it was hopeless.

While Melody struggled to swallow, Brad monologued. His voice was a steady hum but the words barely registered in her mind. She forced herself to nod along, trying to look interested as she chewed, even though each bite made her stomach churn. She bit her lip to steady herself, but the taste of blood only made things worse.

"Are you okay?" Brad asked, when he finally noticed Melody holding back a gag.

"Mmhmm" she grunted back, forcing herself to gulp down the mess. He looked relieved at her quick recovery and resumed his rambling.

Melody tuned him out, focusing instead on his chiselled jawline and perfectly tousled hair. The fact that she was on a date with one of the most popular boys at school was exciting. She had almost lost herself in the rhythm of his voice when his question yanked her back to reality.

"So, do you think you could hook me up with those tickets?" Brad's tone was casual, but he leaned in, eyes bright with anticipation. "You know, since your dad's a big deal in the music industry and all."

Melody blinked at him, realization hitting her like a slap to the face. Of course, that's why he had asked her out. Not because he liked her or wanted to get to know her, but because he wanted something from her. Disappointment mingled with the nausea roiling in her gut.

"I don't think I can help you with that," she said with a grimace.

Brad's expression darkened, the charming smile dropping from his face. "What do you mean you can't help? Your dad's a big shot. He could get those tickets, no problem. What's the big deal?"

Melody opened her mouth to respond, but a rotten burp came out instead. Brad's face twisted in disgust. He leaned forward, his voice rising. "Forget it. This was a waste of time. Everyone knows you're a freak, but this was your way out. If you're gonna be a little bitch about it though, then fuck you."

Melody's eyes grew, shocked by his unexpected anger. She stammered, trying to say something to defuse the situation, while people at nearby tables stared at the commotion. Brad shoved his chair back, the legs screeching against the floor, while Melody sank into her seat to hide from the stares of the other diners.

Embarrassed, she realized a boy about her age was setting down a tray of drinks at a nearby table and storming over. He had a confident stride, dark messy hair falling into his eyes, and a leer that hinted he was ready for a fight.

"Is everything okay here?" His voice was calm, but there was a firmness to it that made Brad pause.

He scowled at the other boy. "This isn't any of your business."

The boy didn't flinch, his gaze steady. "It is if you're making a scene in my restaurant."

Brad looked at the boy like he might explode, with his fists clenched at his sides, and jaw held tight. Melody saw the distraction as her opportunity to escape, but Brad noticed her attempt to slink away, and with one final glare he stormed out of the restaurant.

The boy turned to her, his expression softening. "You okay?"

Melody nodded, embarrassed but grateful for his rescue. "I'll be fine. Thanks."

He smiled, making her heart skip a beat. "Don't mention it. That guy's a jerk."

"Yeah, he is."

At that, she grabbed her bag, and started towards the door, but before she could leave, the boy lightly touched her arm, stopping her.

"Leaving so soon?" he asked softly.

Melody hesitated, glancing at the people gawking at her and typing furiously into their phones. This scene would be instant gossip fodder for their entire high school. "Yeah, I think I've had enough for one night."

He raised an eyebrow. "Why not stay a bit? Make sure that guy isn't waiting outside to continue the fight. I'll keep you company."

She sighed, torn. She didn't want to stay, but she wasn't ready to go home yet and have to explain to her parents why she was back so soon. Nodding, she let the boy lead her to a new spot at the counter.

"I don't even know your name."

"Jake," he told her, holding out his hand.

"Melody," she replied, shaking it. His grip was warm and comforting.

"Nice to meet you, Melody," Jake said, his eyes holding hers.

As Jake moved around the diner, taking orders and dropping off food, he stopped by to chat with Melody whenever he had a moment. He was funny, teasing her in a light-hearted way that put her at ease. Every time he smiled at her, a bit more of the tension from her disastrous date melted away.

Melody sipped on a soda, even though it turned sour in her mouth. Jake would walk by say something witty, flash that charming smile of his, or touch her softly, and she'd get distracted, forgetting about the curse until the next rancid sip reached her tongue.

The hours passed quickly, and soon the diner was empty. Jake leaned against the counter, arms crossed. "You've been a trooper tonight."

She laughed, surprised by the sound. "Well, I guess I owed you after you rescued me from that disaster."

Jake shrugged, still smiling. "Happy to help. Besides, it's not every night I get to hang out with a girl as cool as you."

Melody's cheeks flushed, and she looked down, trying to hide them. "Thanks, Jake. This was fun."

His eyes sparkled with mischief in response. "The night's not over yet. Want to help me clean up?"

Melody hesitated, but then nodded. "Sure."

They fell into an easy rhythm. He showed her how to wipe down the tables, sweep the floors, and stack the chairs, all while keeping up a steady stream of chatter. Melody found herself laughing more than she had in a long time. Jake was gorgeous, and funny, and Melody couldn't remember the last time she felt this comfortable around anyone, let alone a boy she had just met.

As they were finishing up, Jake asked, "So, what was the deal with that guy earlier? He doesn't seem like your type."

Melody hesitated, unsure how much to share. "He's…not. I guess I was just trying to fit in. Do something normal for once. I'm not exactly popular at school."

Jake nodded thoughtfully. "I get that. But normal is overrated. Popular sucks."

"You're probably right." She said, relieved.

They finished closing up in companionable silence. With the restaurant clean, and the lights dimmed, the only sound was the distant hum of the refrigerators in the kitchen.

"Want to do the honors?" he asked, gesturing to the garbage by the back door.

Melody laughed as she picked up a bag. "Lead the way."

Jake showed Melody to the dumpster, where they threw in the trash bags. They stood there for a moment in silence, then Jake turned to her, his expression soft. "Thanks for keeping me company tonight. I had a really good time with *you*."

Melody's heart raced. "I should be the one thanking you."

Jake didn't say anything else but inched closer. Before she could process what was happening, he leaned in and kissed her. It was gentle and brief, but it was her first kiss, and it made her toes curl. For a moment, everything was perfect.

But then the panic set in. What if her curse somehow affected him? She pulled back, her breath hitching in her throat.

Jake looked at her, concern flickering in his eyes.

"That bad of a kiss, eh?"

Melody shook her head. "No, no! Just... nervous, I guess."

Jake brushed a strand of hair from her face. "Don't be. I really liked it."

She breathed, trying to calm her racing heart. They stood there for a moment, and then Jake stepped back, giving her some space.

"My ride will be here soon. Can I give you a lift home?" he asked.

"Oh, that's okay. I live right down the street and biked here."

"Okay, will you text me when you get home though?"

She said of course, and they exchanged numbers. After a quick hug goodbye, and another kiss on Melody's cheek, she hopped on her bike to head home. Melody felt a strange mix of excitement and dread. Everything seemed fine, but as she peddled away, she thought she heard Jake let out a small cough.

***

Melody walked through the front door, texting Jake "Made it home".

Her parents were in the family room, the glow of the television casting shadows across their faces. Her mom looked up, smiling warmly.

"How was your night, sweetheart?"

Melody forced a smile back. "It was good. A bit strange, but good."

Her dad looked over with mild concern. "Strange how?"

Melody shrugged, trying to downplay the weirdness of the evening. "Just different. But I met a nice guy."

Her mom's smile widened. "That's wonderful, honey. Want to join us for a cup of tea before bed?"

The thought of consuming anything else made Melody's stomach turn, but she didn't want to worry her parents. "Sure, I'll have a little."

She sat down with them, accepting the cup her mom handed her. The steam curled upward, filling her nostrils with the comforting scent of chamomile. But as she took a sip, the tea soured, chunks of dirt and tea leaves sprinkled throughout, and she struggled to swallow the dry bitter mess.

***

Later, as she lay in bed, her mind raced with thoughts of Jake, their kiss, and the cough he let out. She tried to dismiss her worries as paranoia, but they gnawed at her until she fell into a nightmare-fueled sleep.

In her dream, Melody sat at the counter of the empty diner, holding an oily glass filled with a thick churning milkshake. Despite her gut urging her to push it away, she raised the glass to her mouth and took a gulp. Maggots within squirmed across her tongue, popping in an explosion of flavour between her teeth. Shocked by how delicious it was, she devoured the concoction.

While she swallowed, groaning with perverted satisfaction, a figure emerged from the shadows. It was Jake, but all wrong; his skin was grey, body gaunt, eyes sunken and bruised.

"Drink up, Melody," Jake rasped, his voice sending chills down her spine. "You know you want to."

She tried to respond, but when she opened her mouth, vomit and insects spilled out. Jake laughed and leaned closer, stretching the cracked skin on his lips across his rotten teeth. It peeled away in spots, revealing raw, festering flesh underneath. "You can't resist it," he whispered with hot and fetid breath. "This is who you are."

Falling, she went to grab Jake to steady herself. Wherever her fingers brushed his skin, it crumbled away like ash. Instead of horror, she felt a surge of desire, a sickening *hunger* that clawed at her insides. The idea of devouring him filled her with a dark, primal thrill.

Jake's body was falling apart, but he pulled her to her feet, his clammy touch sending heat through her body. "Let's dance," he murmured, pulling her close.

They began swaying slowly to the rhythm of her racing heart. Jake's flesh continued to slough off in chunks that hit the floor with wet, sickening thuds. But Melody didn't pull away; she was captivated by the sight of him decaying in her arms.

With every turn, the diner morphed. The walls leaked a thick, black ooze, and the floor rotted away, revealing a dark void beneath them. But none of it mattered to Melody. All she could focus on was the boy in her arms, his flesh disintegrating with every movement, the smell of death clinging to him like cologne. Her fingers traced the line of his jaw, leaving a trail of bubbled and blistered skin in their wake.

"Do you like what you see?" Jake's voice was tender with affection.

Melody leaned in, her body craving the destruction of his flesh. She wanted to *taste* him. Desperate, she pressed her lips to his cold and wet ones, feeling them dissolve under the pressure. He shoved his tongue into her mouth and she loved the way it tasted as she chewed it into a pulp. His whole body began to fall apart then, arms crumbling away, torso collapsing into a festering pile. Yet she kept kissing him, her mouth filling with the taste of decay, drowning in twisted satisfaction.

***

She woke with a start, drenched in sweat. The dream clung to her, the taste of rot still lingering on her tongue, Jake's crumbling flesh still imprinted on her lips. She was horrified by how turned on it made her feel.

Her phone buzzed, pulling her back to reality. Trembling, she saw Jake's name and a message: "Glad you made it home safe. Want to meet up again tomorrow?"

She hesitated, replaying the nightmare in her mind. But it was just her imagination running wild. Jake was fine, and he wanted to see her again.

"I'd love to. When and where?"

His reply came almost instantly. "How about the park by the river? After I get off my shift around 6."

"Awesome, see you there."

Tomorrow would be different. She would push aside the curse and enjoy being with someone who made her feel normal. But the dream had felt so real, so visceral, and the hunger it had awakened in her still lingered in the back of her mind.

***

The afternoon sun dipped low as Melody walked to the park. As nightmare faded into the background, it was replaced by nervous excitement about seeing Jake again. He was waiting for her on a bench near the water, head tilted down as he scrolled through his phone.

His shaggy hair blew in the wind, and she giggled a little in wonder at how hot he was. But as she got closer her excitement dimmed—Jake didn't look right. His skin was pale, with dark circles under his eyes, his posture slumped and movement sluggish.

"Hey," she called out softly, voice filled with concern. "Are you feeling okay?"

Jake looked up, his expression momentarily unreadable. He managed a smile that didn't quite reach his eyes. "Yeah, I'm fine. A little under the weather. Probably just a cold."

Melody frowned, worry deepening. "Are you sure? We can totally reschedule."

Jake waved her concern away. "I'm fine. A little tired after back-to-back shifts, but I didn't want to cancel on you."

His words were reassuring, but there was something about his tone that made her skin prickle with unease. Still, she forced a smile, not wanting to spoil their date. "Okay, but if you start feeling worse, let me know, alright?"

He nodded, standing up from the bench. "Promise. I've been looking forward to this."

They walked along the river, conversation flowing easily. Melody found herself relaxing, and they talked about everything from their favourite movies to their most embarrassing stories. There were moments when he seemed to falter—his face paling even more, and a ragged cough hacking his lungs—but each time he quickly brushed it off, insisting he was fine.

As darkness fell, they found themselves wandering through a secluded area of the park, with dense trees. The sound of the river bubbling nearby created a serene backdrop. Melody felt so content, last night's dream and her curse and Jake's cough were all momentarily forgotten.

They stopped by a large tree, its gnarled roots twisting up from the ground. Jake turned to face her, his expression serious.

"I'm really glad we did this," he said quietly.

"Me too." Melody replied as she looked into his eyes, anticipating what was coming next.

Jake stepped closer, gently tucking a strand of hair behind her ear. She leaned into him, breath hitching. Slowly, he bent down, his lips hovering above hers for a moment, and then he kissed her. It was soft at first, tentative, as if they were both still testing the waters. But as the seconds ticked by, it deepened, and Melody melted into him, arms wrapping around his neck as she lost herself in the moment. The world around them faded away.

Then, Melody felt a sharp pain in her side. She gasped, pulling back in confusion, her eyes widening as she looked down to see Jake's hand gripping a small, glinting knife, its blade buried in her side.

"Jake?" Her voice was barely a whisper, her mind struggling to comprehend.

Jake's face hardened as he pulled the knife out and stepped back. Melody staggered, clutching at her side, as blood seeped through her fingers, warm and sticky. It wasn't the pain that shocked her the most though—it was the cold, detached look in Jake's eyes.

"This is how it has to be Melody," he said, his voice devoid of any kindness.

Stunned, Melody stumbled. "What? Why are you doing this?"

Jake sighed, disappointed. "You thought I didn't know what you were?"

Melody fell to the ground, trying to back away and shaking her head no.

Jake voice grew low and dangerous. "You're a Cursed One. And it's my job to stop you."

A chill went down her spine, fear and anger warring within her. "Stop me? What are you talking about?"

Jake's expression twisted into something angry. "Your curse, Melody. Did you think everyone was just eating maggots and not saying anything?"

Melody started to sob.

"Your parents made a deal with the devil. They brought you into this world so they could have money and success, but your very existence will destroy us all." Jake continued, clearly enjoying his little history lesson. "You aren't the first, and you won't be the last. My family is part of an organization that's been around for generations, tasked with saving humanity and stopping those like you."

Melody's mind reeled. "That doesn't make any sense, my parents are good people, *normal* people! And I would never hurt anyone!"

"Of course they wanted you to think that. But we've been tracking you for months, and we know the truth. It starts with food, but it will get so much worse. Everything you touch will start to fall apart, and eventually the whole world will end. So now, I have to end you instead." His voice softening slightly. "I did like hanging out with you, but I don't have a choice. It's either you or everyone else."

Rage and fear surged through Melody, giving her strength despite the pain in her side. She loved her parents. She had trusted Jake. And now he was telling her that they were liars, and he had planned to kill her all along.

"I'm not going to let you do this," she spat, her voice trembling.

Jake stepped closer, raising the knife again. "I'm sorry, Melody, but it's already done."

When he moved in for another strike, she lunged, using every ounce of willpower she had left. The speed of her attack caught him off guard, and they both went tumbling to the ground. The knife skittered out of his hand, and Melody quickly scrambled for it, hands slick with her own blood.

Before she could grab it, Jake was on her again, his hands around her throat, squeezing tight. She gasped for air, her vision swimming, but refused to give up. With a desperate surge of energy, she brought her knee up, hard, connecting with his balls. He grunted in pain, and fell to the side, allowing Melody to roll on top of him. She yanked his hair, smashing his head into the roots of the tree they landed on repeatedly until his eyes clouded over. Remembering a move from the self-defence lessons in her gym class, she pushed her thumbs into his eye sockets, and felt them sink into the squishy tissue as he screamed.

In that moment, something changed. Melody was no longer scared—she was *starving*. Time seemed to slow, as she took her thumbs into her mouth, sucking the delicious juices off. She realized what she had to do, the only way this could end with her survival, and she wanted to do it.

Bending close to Jake's face, she whispered, "Best dinner date ever" and bit into on his throat as hard as she could.

GIFTS OF LIFE

JF FOSTER

When I met Daddy, I thought I knew where the line was. The line that separated the acceptable—ending at a bit questionable—from the truly gross. Then he taught me that, like many things, *gross* is just a construct.

Daddy took me home on the night we first met. I was celebrating the end of my university exams with a few friends, when, from the darkness of the nightclub, he appeared. Hulking, easily a foot taller than me, and even in the poor lighting, his light eyes glistened. He asked if I wanted to dance—I did. I was amazed he would pick me, chubby and plain, out of the preening flocks of twinks and bullish muscle bottoms, practically *presenting* to him hoping to be picked. I felt so special.

The music pumped, and I felt a shiver down my spine as his rough hands caressed my soft curves. I stared at his muscular body, wishing to be crushed against him. I inhaled his pungent scent. We didn't need names, he told me when I asked him on the sidewalk later. He commanded me to call him *Daddy* or *Sir* and, in return, he would call me *Boy*.

When the music cut, Daddy brought me to a sparsely decorated unit in a nearby high-rise. The kitchen was seemingly empty, while in the main room, the few pieces of nondescript furniture were pushed flush against the walls around the central space; bare aside from a lone concrete support pillar. It was hard to imagine this was somebody's home. Maybe it wasn't, I thought. A hotel maybe, or he was so rich that this was just a part-time place not worth investing the effort to personalize.

Across the front of the unit, a broad stretch of tall windows revealed a breathtaking view of the city, the mountains and the waters beyond. Even as Daddy ordered me to strip naked for inspection, I was mesmerized. What a place to get fucked. I quivered with anticipation, nearly moaning when I felt his hands on my back.

"Didn't expect anyone to take you home, did you, Boy?" he growled, patting my plump behind.

"No," I giggled.

He slapped my ass, hard.

"No what, Boy?"

"No, *Sir*."

"Good Boy."

I felt a pinching sensation; he was beginning to press inside me. Even his fingers were thick. It was impossible to stay quiet as he inserted one, then two. I gasped when he eventually removed both. There was a moment of silence before he flashed the fingers in front of my face: they were streaked with brown.

At that moment I wished for death.

"Don't worry, it happens all the time," he growled gently. My heart ached as, with his clean hand, he reached out and ruffled my hair affectionately.

I wanted to ask about a shower, but when I started to speak, Daddy shushed me. He ordered me onto my hands and knees. My eyes widened, but his tone was clear. I turned away and lowered myself, feeling the cool tile beneath my hands, taking in the city.

In the reflection ahead of me, I watched Daddy's enormous form undress. Pale and muscular, dense dark fur streaked with white covered his shoulders and chest. I watched a wolfish grin bloom as he lowered to claim his prize. Meaty hands grasped my waist tightly, and I cried out. Daddy was *big*.

Slowly, he began rocking back and forth. After a few moments, my nose twitched.

Shit.

The smell was faint at first, but as his strokes quickened, the stench quickly grew overpowering. My eyes watered. It was Daddy's exuberant moans of pleasure that kept me going. It wasn't bothering him, so I steeled myself and inhaled deeply, willing myself to take in the deep complexities, and give myself wholly.

The fecal aroma filled the room, until finally, with a yell, I felt Daddy erupt deep inside me before quickly pulling out and stumbling to lean against the cement pillar. He pointed me to the bathroom to start a shower; he would be there soon.

As the shower sputtered to life, I grimaced. Filthy brown ran down my legs.

Minutes later, Daddy joined me. For the first time, I noticed a tattoo on his torso, tracing the v-line above his member. A beast with wild horns; one pair curling downward, and a second flaring up, peaking out from the brown smears around his crotch--like he had been fucking a chocolate pudding cup. A ram, he told me. It looked good, but… something about the ram's black-and-white gaze—the way it was drawn, I suppose—unnerved me.

My nose must have wrinkled at the shit covering us, because Daddy let out a low chuckle and reached out to rub my shoulders. I couldn't hide the glow of satisfaction that emanated from me the rest of that week, prompting questions from the few friends also staying in the city for the summer. Coyly, I told them I had met someone.

Daddy sent me a text the next weekend. He wanted my throat—was I ready? I rushed over after dinner with friends, desperate for his approval. That night he impaled me, forcing me viciously eye to eye with the ram until I was gagging and writhing. I finally managed to escape, and in the same motion hurled my meal—a Cactus Club Thai noodle bowl—across him. He uttered a hoarse groan. Gasping for air, I watched him reach a hand into the mess and begin rubbing it across his furry chest. Closed his eyes, Daddy ordered me to continue my sloppy service.

"Good Boy," he later rasped, as fat globs of ejaculate landed noisily in the mire. I must have done a *very* good job, because he promised to take me out for our next date.

The following Friday, he and I arrived at the most elegant restaurant I had ever been in. Under the cover of the live string quartet, while I suppressed the urge to stare in wonder at the lush draping and art lining the room, Daddy explained that he got off on celebrating parts of the human experience that others shunned; the taboos that we try to hide from ourselves as much as the world around us.

"For all the sticky, smelly *insides* of it all," His pale eyes danced in the candlelight, "the body is a wonderland—or a water park." His booming laugh attracted banal glares. "Some people get off on drinking sperm and piss. Or love getting their pubes soaked by some sloppy head. Just because it's not mainstream doesn't mean it's *bad*. Grossness is just the far side of a line boring people are loath to cross."

And if I wanted, he could show me.

Staring into his steely eyes, I burned; the topic was so at odds with the surroundings, but I couldn't deny the swelling in my pants. The thought of Daddy thinking *I* was one of those boring people was unbearable.

"Yes, Sir."

I readily accepted as Daddy opened me to the pleasure that came from embracing our natural fluids. The human body is a disgusting thing, all of us subject to its whims: shitting and pissing like clockwork, vomiting when we're sick and pustulating when we need to heal. According to Daddy, these things were the very gifts of life. Gifts to us, and from us to each other. It was almost romantic to be willing to give oneself to the other so wholly.

Over the first few weeks of our relationship, it was so refreshing to be with him—so free of the usual nerves and shame that came with exploring a new partner's body. I perfected the timing of when to eat to ensure I was full enough for his desires. Some days he was in the mood to drench me in throat slime, while others he wanted my waste, usually as a messy lube, but also occasionally to paint me with it or, one time, tasting it. One night, I had to drink his bladderful of stinking urine, which I promptly upchucked over myself. We did everything imaginable in a blur of the best sex of my young life.

It lasted most of the summer, until Daddy mentioned adding a third for the first time one night during Pride. I was mortified. He's over me, my panicked mind screamed. He found someone hotter, who can give him more than me. Sensing my feelings, Daddy held me and stroked my hair. His chest rumbled as he told me what we had was special, but an alpha like him needed more than just one boy. Didn't I want Daddy to have what he deserved? I did, so I relented, though a cold lump had taken up residence in my throat.

On my iPhone, I created a fresh Grindr account under a fake email. We took a quick snap of our naked torsos, and I set the username to *daddy+boy 4 (vomiting emoji)*. Within minutes of the profile going live, we heard a *blip*— our first message. We fielded offers for a while, eventually agreeing on a slender twunk. He and I took turns pleasing Daddy, gifting him all we had until all three of us lay in a heap on the protective tarp, covered in juices and gasping with lusty wonder.

Nights with Daddy began featuring a rotating cast—either he would share me with other daddies, or find a boy to join me. But, regardless of who was present, the scents, the textures and the warmth of fresh gifts were constant and overflowing—a veritable slip'n'slide of chunks.

By the time my classes were starting back up, Daddy was insatiable. He wanted to meet nearly every night, and my holes were growing raw from sheer use. I needed a break, but even the idea of letting Daddy down made me want to cry. I was high on pleasure, and continued, without fail, to heed his beck and call. If I had just ghosted and disappeared, then what happened next could have been avoided. Or at least delayed to another day. With another boy.

But I didn't, and it wasn't.

I could tell that September evening that Daddy was in a mood. Throughout dinner, he was twitchy, barely listening to a word I said about my new term schedule. Instead his ice-chip eyes roved the room hungrily. Afterwards, we went to the club—the same one we had met at months ago. He led me past the bumping line, nodding at the bouncer, but once inside, Daddy abandoned me almost immediately.

Sulking, I grabbed a drink and found a seat near the bar, bobbing my head in time with the music. A few guys tried to talk to me but I blew them off, focused instead on Daddy as he stalked the dance floor, occasionally stopping to talk to some hot young thing or other. Of course—none of them looked like me. These were the beautiful ones, with abs, jawlines and confidence. I should have left—I'm sure he wouldn't have noticed.

It wasn't until after midnight that Daddy finally found me, leading a slender guy with dark features. The twink threw me a nervous grin, and introducing himself as Alex. The smile I gave in return was anything but warm. I withheld my name. I didn't bother getting to know the other boys.

Daddy rushed us back to his condo. As soon as we crossed his threshold, us boys were ordered to strip while he set out the tarp. Goosebumps rippled across my back as I exposed my flesh to the chilly unit.

Things started out as normal: the other boy and I took turns licking and sucking Daddy, covering him and each other with the contents of our stomachs. When we were good and wet, Daddy grabbed me by the jaw and forced my gaze upward. It hurt, but I didn't protest. Staring deep into my eyes, he asked if I had brought him any other gifts tonight.

"Yes, Sir," I moaned, feeling pressure in my bowels.

Daddy's thick fingers caressed my cheek. Eyes still on me, he barked at the other boy to lay on the ground. The twink wavered, looking at the puddles of orange-beige around us.

"Did I stutter, Boy?"

A smirk toyed at my lips: I knew never to make Daddy ask a second time.

Daddy started to stroke himself as our guest star obeyed. He watched hungrily as the slender boy lay down. Straddling him, I lowered into a squat over his chest. Daddy's breathing grew ragged as comprehension dawned in the other boy's eyes. He squirmed in protest, but stilled at Daddy's bark. I almost felt sorry for Alex as he pushed himself back down, a look of disgust on his face.

Hovering a few inches above, I gulped and looked away. Instead, I locked eyes with the ever-watching ram from its place over Daddy's pumping hand. Inhaling deeply, I tightened my abdomen, until I felt warm relief. My breath quickened. Fecal perfume rose as my bowels loosed over the boy's smooth torso in a series of satisfying *plops*. Music to Daddy's ears, I knew—we'd done this one before. This guest would leave and then I'd get pounded to the edge of my life. Between my legs, my cock stood at attention.

When I was finished, Daddy dismissed me with a wave of his hand. He twitched for a moment, and groaned as a stream of urine spouted forth, splattering over the twink. It smelled nearly as strongly as the brown sludge.

Pitifully squirming in the mire, the twink pulled up onto his elbows.

"Stay down," Daddy snarled.

Alex ignored him. He made to stand. "...*gross*," he muttered.

Daddy froze. Blanched in the glow of the moon and the city, he seemed like a still image. Every muscle etched into relief by the dark fur, each streak of white radiating the same message of age and power. His eyes—those eyes that had been so beautiful—were alight with a dreadful, molten fury, his teeth bared in a bestial grimace.

He took a single step.

Then rushed.

I backed out of the way, tumbling onto a white leather sofa. Daddy grabbed the twink's throat, cutting him off with a squawk. The young man's eyes bulged with terror. Daddy pulled him across the room. A pleading gaze met mine, but I could only sit where I fell and watch, my mouth agape.

"We told you what to expect," Daddy rumbled. His muscles were swollen. "Don't blame me if you can't handle our *gifts*, you ungrateful little shit." He wound back and—

CRACK.

The twink's skull met the concrete pillar. I saw the light of life flit from Alex's eyes into oblivion and retched. His cranium collapsed inward and the body fell limp in Daddy's grasp.

Neither of us spoke, as if maintaining the void of silence prevented the truth from being brought into reality. With horror, I stood and edged toward Daddy. I hoped I would see regret on his face. I hoped that, as he stared around at the pulpy mess and the splattered and gushing red, he would panic like a child. But my hope was pointless. I nearly gagged at what I did see.

My footsteps splashed in the accumulated muck. Daddy reached an exploratory hand up and, suddenly, plunged a finger through the blood-soaked hair, emitting a grotesque cry of ecstasy. When he pulled his hand back, a sharp tearing rent the air. Between his fingers, I could see the scraps of skin and hair attached to the small fragment of bone. Daddy looked from the body to me.

"C'mere Boy," he whispered. A silvery tone entered his voice.

He waggled his still-firm member. I would have done anything to be anywhere else. But I wasn't. My heart pounded, and I knelt down to serve Daddy.

As I sucked, I pretended not to notice Daddy further desecrating the broken boy, bits of skull falling into the mess around me. The ram's wicked gaze bore into me. Observing this horror was too much. I closed my eyes and focused single-mindedly on my task, but when Daddy let out a deafening moan, I couldn't help peeking up. His hand was deep in the twinks ruined brain, rifling around the braincase like Satan's cookie jar. Each push of his cock down my throat and was matched by his fingers into grey matter. He roared in ecstasy.

Minutes passed until I heard, "Give me your ass, Boy."

I paused—though not long enough for Daddy to ask again—and got in position. There was a *squelch* above me and my stomach dropped. Worse still was the loud thump and splash. I looked back to see Daddy, a lump of grey in his palm, which he began slathering over his turgid length. Alex's body lay discarded in the muck, off to the side. I endured what came next, focusing on the sensation but doing anything I could to evade reality deep inside myself. Thankfully, Daddy didn't last long. After a few minutes he let out a cry.

I pulled myself free of him. Without bothering to wash away the layer of filth, I pulled my clothes on and made some excuse to leave. The last thing I saw as the door swung shut was Daddy, one hand was on his crotch, the other reaching out toward the twink. The corpse.

Nope. I slammed the door shut and left as quickly as I could.

I raced home under the full moon, arriving wet, reeking of shit and vomit. The night swirled through my mind as I scrubbed myself clean and douched for a second time, hoping to exorcise any remnants of brain up in me. My flesh ached when I finally curled into bed, shivering between the clammy sheets. Before sleep claimed me I was struck with the desperate hope that I was hallucinating, that there was never an Alex to begin with, and what Daddy had done was some fucked-up dream.

The next day I stumbled through my classes like a zombie, haunted by the image of the collapsed skull and dead eyes. The idea of going to Daddy's place made me sick, but I knew he would expect me after my final lecture let out. If I didn't show up, I knew he'd seek me out—Daddy knew where I lived, where I worked. And I couldn't hide on campus forever.

The condo was spotless when I arrived. At first, nothing was awry, but as I undid my shoes, I was struck by a sharp tang in the air I couldn't identify. Daddy's voice emanated from the ensuite. I hadn't been in there before, only the second bathroom with its minimalist shower stall. Trepidatious, I crept through the dark bedroom toward the sliver of light. What I saw when I moved through the cracked door was definitely not a hallucination.

The liquid filling the tub was blinding against the white marble tile. Shiny scarlet covered Daddy from the belly down. More blood than what came from one body, I thought, my stomach turning.

Daddy commanded me to join him. I stripped—fighting myself the entire time—and stepped into the thick, tepid liquid. Red ripples lapped at the edge of the tub as I rode him.

Voice low, he whispered in my ear urgently, as my breathing picked up and my body relaxed onto his throbbing horn. We had an opportunity to go into uncharted territory—Daddy and Boy, exploring together. Sure, vomit, piss and shit were great, but we've gone to our limits. To enjoy the full variety of human pleasures, we had to go boldly where most feared to tread. When we finally both shot into the scarlet depths, I felt so connected to him.

We shared a dark secret, after all.

"But won't we get caught, Sir?" I panted. Daddy laughed darkly. Someone must have seen Alex leave with us from the club. It was only a matter of time before something led to us.

"There's not a chance m'boy," a bloody hand stroked my arm. I was so small next to his bulky, hairy frame. "I've got too much weight behind me for that to happen." He refused to elaborate, instead suggesting I rinse off and go back home to cool off. "After a good sleep you'll see that really, nothing at all has changed."

As I stepped onto the darkening street, panic filled me again. That night I fell into an uneasy sleep, and dreamed of Daddy and I dancing in the moonlight. Beyond the edge of the clearing I heard whoops and calls from unseen spectators—come to save me perhaps? We twirled and I strained to catch a glimpse, but every time I came close, Daddy pulled me tighter to whisper soft assurances. Finally I managed to rip free of him, and raced to a rustling thicket, desperate for whatever help the voices could offer. I let out a shriek at what lay within the foliage. Staring back was Alex. Sweet pink brains peaked out from the caved in skull. Shit and blood poured from his lips as soundlessly, he asked, *Why?*

Behind me Daddy loomed. Horns grew from his head: one pair curled down to his jaw, while the second glimmered threateningly against the starry sky.

I woke, sweating and gasping, I knew I couldn't go back to Daddy. Not today. Not for a while. Maybe not ever. I thought about turning him in, or blocking and ghosting. I really did. But if I went to the police would they even believe me? I didn't know Daddy's name, or anything about Alex. They'd dismiss me as a hysterical faggot. Plus, nobody knew me so well. Who else would understand why I wanted to vomit on them, or would be willing to *defile* me the way I wanted in the name of pure pleasure? And so, like an addict, I returned to Daddy merely three days later, haggard from desire.

Things couldn't get worse, I had thought, but I quickly saw how wrong I was. The main room was alight, the evening sun reflecting on pools of filth. A wall of stink met me—not feces, I realized with a second whiff. Something deeper…fouler.

Sat on the floor, leaned up against the concrete pillar, was Daddy. He was in the middle of pleasuring himself with something chunky—a silicone toy, I prayed.

"So nice of you to join us, Boy," he rasped, only looking at me when the door shut with a *thud*. It sounded like he hadn't spoken in days. Perhaps since I'd last seen him. "The more, the merrier."

That's when I noticed them. Not one dead twink, but two.

Against the wall, a lithe body dangled limply like a marionette from slick purple ropes; intestines, spilled from a torn belly, wrapped around appendages. The form was held up on hooks that hadn't been there during my last visit.

The other twink was in even worse, sprawled across the floor. Or, at least, part of him was. The head was missing. Instead, a bloody stump of neck faced me. The hole that formerly functioned as an esophagus was stretched open.

I gagged. This wasn't happening.

"Any hole is a goal." Daddy chuckled darkly, continuing to play with the beige mass.
I nearly vomited as the depraved scene completed itself.

It was the detached head, clutched firmly in Daddy's thick hands, with his penis inserted into the mouth. The flushed tip bobbed through the ruined edge of the throat. Black hair waved uselessly, while eyes stared into the chasm of his unholy taint. The ram looked on hungrily.

What happened next was a blur. I lost my cool: I remember yelling, accusing, and threatening. I remember a flick crunch as Daddy stood and hurled the decapitated head at the wall. The door was so far away then, and it was hard to manoeuvre the slippery floor. I remember the feeling of Daddy's hand on my neck and his voice grating my ears while he berated me. His muscles pulled me along easily, as he slammed me into the wall once, then twice, and then…

And then black.

The well wasn't there yesterday. It hadn't been there for any of the twenty-two years that Daniel lived in the house. It was here today.

Daniel stared at the well from the kitchen window. A hallucination, maybe? A dream. He lightly slapped his face. Ow. Not a dream. There was a stone water well in his backyard, with a little roof and everything. A crank that led to an implied bucket. Like in a story.

He walked outside through the back door and stared at the well. Yup, it was still there. Stared at the well for a little longer. Mason, Daniel's son, opened the back door and walked up to him. He looked where Daniel was looking.

"Is that a well?"

"Looks like it," Daniel said.

"Where'd it come from?" Mason asked.

"Dunno." They stared together. It was nice. It was the longest amount of time he'd spent with his son since his wife (and Daniel's mother) passed away three months ago.

"Weird," Mason said. Daniel didn't say anything. He just enjoyed the moment.

o

Mason walked up to the well and looked inside.

"Be careful."

"I can't see the bottom," Mason said.

"Be careful," Daniel repeated. "That means it's really deep." Mason looked at his Dad and sighed. He was twelve and sighed a lot these days.

"I will, Dad."

"I'm just saying."

Mason tried to turn the crank on the side of the well, but it wouldn't move.

"I think it's stuck," he said.

"Let me try." Daniel tried to turn the crank. It did seem to be stuck. Then Daniel heard a soft, disgusting *squelch* echo from the well and the crank started to turn.

The bucket was heavy. Heavier than Daniel thought a bucket of water would be. When the bucket reached the top, they both stared at it. The sides of the bucket were slick, but not with water. It looked slimy. Daniel looked into the bucket and winced.

"It's some kind of … goop," Daniel said.

"Wait a second." Mason ran back into the house. Daniel didn't move. Something was wrong. The bucket swung slightly side to side and the goop jiggled.

(o)

Mason returned wearing a pair of plastic, yellow kitchen gloves.

"Where did you get those?"

"They were under the sink," Mason said. "Mom bought them but never used them."

"Oh." He didn't know what else to say. "Be careful."

"I know, Dad." Mason grabbed the bucket and slowly pulled it towards him. He placed it on the ground and the goop jiggled. It was an opaque and muddy magenta. Daniel thought the goop looked like filthy Jello.

"Wow," Mason said. He leaned over and started to tilt the bucket. Daniel didn't even consider telling Mason not to. He wanted to see what would happen. The goop started to pour out of the bucket with the consistency of melted taffy, or syrup, and the surface changed from opaque to mostly translucent. Daniel could now see what was inside the goop.

"What the fuck?" he said.

"Language, Dad," Mason told him.

Hair. Teeth. What looked like fingernails. Inside the goop. Mason either didn't notice or didn't care. Daniel gagged and tried to stop himself from throwing up. There wasn't any noticeable smell, and for some reason that worried Daniel.

"What is it?" Mason asked.

"I don't know," Daniel said. Mason held the bucket upside-down, trying to pour all the liquid from the bucket. The residue stuck to the bottom and stayed there. The goop on the ground jiggled ominously. "Maybe this isn't such a good idea."

Then the goop proved Daniel right. It started to move. It started to *change*.

((o))

The goop, spread out over the grass, gathered itself and started to condense into a sphere. Like a time-lapse of an ice cube in reverse, but violent; it twisted and roiled, bubbles forming and popping as if it was boiling in the open air.

"Um," Daniel said.

"Dad, what's happening?"

The contortions slowed and stopped. Then the sphere's surface solidified and turned opaque again, obscuring the human detritus hidden within. The goop now looked like the glitter slime that Mason's mother had bought him a couple of times, the size of a child's basketball.

"Huh," Daniel said.

Two, stubby little nubs appeared on the bottom of the sphere. It took Daniel a moment to realize what they were. Legs.

"Dad?"

Two smaller orbs emerged from the front of the sphere, changing color from muddy magenta to white, with black circles in the center. Eyes. Like the googly eyes Mason used in art class, except the pupils didn't move. They might as well have been painted on.

"Dad?" Mason said again. The creature—Daniel could no longer call it just *goop*—turned its head to look at Daniel. He stared at it. The creature turned to look at Mason, and then started to waddle towards him with its stubby legs. It fell almost immediately, as if it didn't know how to use them.

"Aww," Mason said. He extended his arms towards it.

"Don't touch it," Daniel advised. Mason ignored him and picked up the creature with the kitchen gloves.

"He's just a goopy lil guy," Mason proclaimed.

"A goopy … little … guy?" Daniel didn't understand.

"Yeah," Mason said. "A goopy lil guy." He held the blob to his chest with one hand and shook the glove off the other. The creature oozed slime that stuck to Mason's shirt. Daniel suppressed another gag. What was the slime made of? What was this creature made of and how did it exist?

"Mason." Words didn't come. He didn't know any. He didn't know how to talk to his son.

"Don't worry, Dad," Mason said. He reached into his pocket with the ungloved hand and took out his phone. "I'm just going to get a selfie really quick and then I'll put him back down."

Daniel shuddered. Mason called it a "him."

(((o)))

Daniel set up tarps in the basement so that the lil guy could stay there without getting his goop all over the rug and furniture.

That's what Mason called him. No name, just "the lil guy." He spent all day downstairs with the lil guy, playing with him and taking selfies. Daniel sat at the kitchen table with his laptop and googled "goop" and all its variations, trying to find out what the hell his son was playing with.

No results.

At bedtime, Mason wanted to take the lil guy up to his room and sleep with him.

"Absolutely not," Daniel said. "We still don't know if it's safe."

"C'mon, Dad," Mason pleaded. "He's just a lil guy! He's not dangerous."

"*Absolutely not*," Daniel repeated.

Later, in bed, Mason excitedly asked his Dad to guess how many likes his selfies with the lil guy were getting.

"I don't know," Daniel said. "Seven?"

"Try a *thousand!*" Mason yelled. His smile was tremendous. Daniel couldn't remember the last time his son had smiled like that.

"Wow. That sounds like a lot."

"It *is* a lot," Mason said, "but we could get more."

"*We?*" Daniel asked, but he'd already turned on his side and closed his eyes. He decided to drop it. "Good night, Mason."

"Night, Dad," Mason said. "I love you."

"Love you too, son."

The next morning, Daniel woke up and went to Mason's room. He wasn't in bed. Daniel went to the kitchen. Then checked the bathroom. Mason wasn't anywhere. Then he remembered.

He walked down to the basement to find Mason aiming his phone at two grotesque, gooey balls of ooze rolling around on the tarps that lined the floor.

"Look, Dad! There's another one!" Daniel stared at the two goop creatures. They stopped in their tracks and stared back with their eyes that didn't move. They jiggled. Daniel shuddered.

((((o))))

"Why did you make another one?" Daniel asked, hours later. Mason aimed his phone at one of the creatures trying to bounce on a mini trampoline that they'd bought for him when he was seven. The creature could *not* bounce; every time it managed to jump, it landed a moment later with a sickening *plop* and stuck to the mat.

"I didn't, Dad."

"Then who did?" He already knew the answer. The first creature had created the second.

"I don't know," Mason said, "but the goopy lil guys are doing numbers."

"Doing … numbers?" Daniel replied. He didn't understand half of what Mason said these days.

"The videos I recorded today already have fifty thousand likes," Mason said. "*Each.*"

"How many videos?"

"Four," Mason admitted, "but I can do another three by dinner. I've gotten eight thousand followers since breakfast, and I can't lose momentum."

"Followers," Daniel repeated. "Momentum."

"Exactly, Dad," Mason said. "You get it."

Daniel did not. Both creatures had stopped walking and turned to look at Daniel. Their eyes did not see. They did not have mouths, and they did not breathe. Their bodies vibrated long after they stopped moving.

"Dad, do you mind? You're making them nervous." Daniel didn't mind. He didn't like the way the creatures looked at him. He left Mason and walked over to the well and stared into it for a very long time.

(((((o)))))

Mason woke Daniel up the next morning before sunrise.

"Dad! The goopy lil guys went viral!" He didn't respond. Mason shook his arm. "Dad! They went viral!"

"What time is it? Go back to sleep."

"The videos have over a million likes!" Daniel opened his eyes. That sounded like a lot.

"That sounds like a lot," he said.

"It is!" Mason replied. "People want their own goopy lil guys! They're saying so!"

"That's great, Mason," Daniel said. He strained to look at his alarm clock. "But go back to sleep. What time is it?"

"I think I have an idea," Mason said.

"What is it?" Daniel replied, but he was already half asleep.

"People want their own lil guys … and there's three of them now … so—"

Daniel sat up. He tried to hide the tremble in his voice, but he knew that Mason could hear it.

"Did you say *three*?"

(((((o)))))

That afternoon, the doorbell rang. No one ever rang the doorbell. Daniel and Rae chose this house because the closest neighbor was two miles away. Night Springs was a small town and everyone kept to themselves. Daniel was pretty sure the doorbell had never been rung before.

The noise startled him. For three hours, Daniel sat and stared at the well and considered the creatures. There were five of them now; things were escalating. The enfolding chaos was increasingly hard to ignore and—the doorbell rang. He stared at the well, and then the doorbell rang again. Daniel finally stood and walked over to the door.

Outside stood a blonde, white woman with dreadlocks talking into a phone screen. She couldn't have been older than nineteen or twenty.

"Hey guys, it's Ashley!" the woman said into her phone. She didn't acknowledge Daniel. "This video is brought to you by Ferros—."

"Hello?"

"Shut up," Ashley said. She didn't look at Daniel and didn't stop smiling. She froze in place for a moment— then the smile broke, and she sighed, looking to the side. "Now I have to do the intro again. Thanks."

"Sorry," Daniel mumbled. A moment passed. Then Ashley's plastic smile reappeared as if a switch had been flipped.

"Hi," she said. "I'm Ashley." She stuck out her hand. Each one of her nails was a different length, a different color, a different shape.

"Okay." He shook Ashley's hand. "I'm Daniel."

"Not Ashley," she said.

"... What?"

"A-S-H-L-E-I-G-H-H," she said. "Ashleighh."

"Okay," Daniel said.

"Two Hs."

"Okay." He had nothing else to say. Another moment passed. They looked at each other. Somewhere, Mason screamed. Daniel whipped his head, expecting to see the creatures attacking his son, expecting to see them ripping and tearing—

"It's Asleighh!" Mason said. He wasn't scared; he was *excited*. His smile, genuine and huge, mirrored Ashleighh's fake one.

She's like the creatures, Daniel thought. *Their eyes don't move—neither does her smile.*

Ashleighh peered past Daniel to see the source of the noise, but instead of seeing Mason, she saw what the lil guys had done to Daniel's home.

Everything was coated in a layer of shiny ooze. One creature, balancing precariously on top of the fridge, fell off and landed on the kitchen tile with a wet *splat*. Another flipped on the garbage disposal while its friend shoved butter knives into its gaping maw. The grinding of metal and the shower of sparks seemed to please the creatures. Another one was inside the fridge, throwing food onto the floor that mixed with the slime. All the food in the fridge was now covered in the creatures' excrement. The last waddled over to Mason and nuzzled against his leg, which was already soaked through with goop.

"The lil guys!" Ashleighh yelled, squealing. She ran to Mason, leaning over to pick up the creature at his feet. The squish that the creature made nauseated Daniel. "I want to buy one! How much?"

"They're, uhh, not for sale," Daniel said. He very much wanted to get rid of the creatures, but he wasn't sure of the legality of selling them from his home.

"Come on, dad," Mason said. "You said it yourself. There's too many of them."

Daniel surveyed the kitchen. There *were* too many, and with their numbers increasing, they were acting more and more unhinged with each new sibling.

"Pretty please?" Ashleighh said. "I'll give you a thousand dollars."

"Cash?" Daniel asked. He didn't trust Ashleighh. Where was she getting a thousand dollars from?

"Do you take Venmo?" Daniel didn't have Venmo on his phone, but Mason showed him how to set it up, and assured him it was legitimate after the funds came through.

"Yay! My followers are going to go fucking nuts! Look at this lil guy!" After checking his Venmo balance again, Daniel ushered Ashleighh out the door, the creature jiggling in her arms, already starting to soak her clothes with ooze.

"Tell your friends," Daniel said, and then shut the door in Ashleighh's face.

((((((o))))))

Ashleighh didn't tell her friends, but she *did* tell her followers, and over the next three days influencers descended on the town of Night Springs. Jaydens and Attysons and Braedyns and Emmahleighs showed up at Daniel's house to get their own goopy lil guys. At first, it unnerved him to have so many people show up at his house, but the money these people with impossible names paid him put him at ease. A little.

They sold four creatures that first day. Mason wanted to keep one and Daniel didn't have the heart to tell him no, so after that, the influencers had to get their own from the well. They liked that; they recorded the process, called them "birthing videos." Daniel didn't mind. For now, the well was still full of goop, and birthed the creatures without complaint.

He sold the first four creatures for a thousand dollars each. The next day, he increased the price to three thousand. The day after that, ten thousand. The influencers were willing to pay, and Daniel was happy to get the creatures out of his house. He didn't think about it too hard.

Jaessika, the last influencer of the second day, set up a tripod to record herself kissing one of the creatures, her saliva and its slime mixing and creating strands of wet goo that connected their faces and refused to break. The strands hung there as she turned back to the camera.

"If you want to see more of me and my lil guy, like and subscribe!" Her face was drenched in goop. It hung from her cheeks in clumps.

On the third day, Daniel saw some unattended creatures separated from their new owners; one carrying a wrench waddling towards the garage, and two more holding butter knives that rolled out of sight when they noticed *him* noticing *them*.

Daniel didn't think too hard about it; he thought about the money instead. Two hundred and thirty thousand dollars. That amount was enough for Daniel to ignore what his life had become. Two hundred and thirty thousand dollars for Mason's college. If he went to college. Mason's future. Daniel didn't understand his son and he wasn't sure if Mason even loved him, but dammit, he was going to take care of him.

It's what Rae would have wanted.

(((((((((o)))))))))

The influencers left Daniel and Mason's house, but they didn't leave Night Springs. It turned out that Night Spring's small-town aesthetic was the perfect backdrop for social media posts. They never shut up about it: Night Spring's *aesthetic*. It didn't matter that Night Springs was real and wanted to be left alone; aesthetic and reality were interchangeable to these people.

Jaysohns walked through the grocery store with selfie sticks, encouraging their creatures to knock over displays; Xachs brought theirs to the dog park and livestreamed all the dogs licking their creatures' unmoving eyes; Summers and Autumns and Wynters brought their lil guys to the movie theater and backlit them with ring lights before letting them run up and down the aisles; all the while, the goop left crisscrossing snail trails across the entire town, making maps with their waste.

Not to mention the alarming appearances of *unchaperoned* creatures: one wandered into the elementary school and jumped into the toilet, clogging it and flooding the entire school; another somehow wormed its way into the engine of one of the town's only two fire trucks, rendering it immobile; yet another was found in the evidence locker at the police station, brandishing a gun.

Daniel sat at the table in the dining room and stared at a picture of Rae on his phone. He listened to Mason watching videos of the people in town with their creatures.

The people of Night Springs *hated* the influencers, and they *hated* the creatures, and they knew the reason why both groups had infested their town, so they also hated Daniel.

On the sixth day, he tried to hire a housekeeper to come and clean up the mess the lil guys had made of his house over the past week. No one returned his calls. He went into town for supplies and the other residents of Night Springs refused to talk to him, refused to even acknowledge him, wouldn't ring him up at the register. He left his bags in the shopping cart and walked back to his car, dejected. The gas station attendant refused to let him put gas in his tank. As he pulled into his driveway, the low fuel light came on.

Now he was stranded at home with Mason and the creature. Mason looked up from his phone for the first time in hours.

"I need to make a video," he said. "My follower count is slipping."

"Okay," Daniel said. It was all he ever said. It was an acknowledgement with no contribution. He had nothing to contribute.

"Where's our lil guy? Have you seen him?"

Daniel didn't know where the creature was, hadn't seen it in hours, and that realization terrified him. He did not acknowledge the terror.

"No," Daniel said. "I haven't." He looked back at his phone, to the picture of Rae.

(((((((((o)))))))))

On the seventh day, Daniel woke to Mason shaking his shoulder, concern draped across his face.

"Is it the creatures?" Daniel asked his son. Mason rolled his eyes.

"No, Dad," Mason said. "There's people here. A lot of them."

"I'll be down in a second." More Elliyiotts and Alyvvias.

"Not influencers," Mason added. "Guys in black vans and suits."

"Shit," Daniel said.

"Language," Mason reminded him.

"I'll be down in a second." Mason gave him a look. "Half a second, I promise."

Two minutes later, Daniel descended the stairs and looked out of the kitchen window, to the well; it had become second nature.

What he saw stopped him in place.

A dozen creatures surrounded the well, lifting and tilting a bucket of goop on to the grass. The ones not involved with the bucket were jumping up and down. Dancing. Their bodies jiggled and shone slick in the sunlight.

They were making more of themselves. A *lot* more.

Then the well and all twelve of the creatures were engulfed in flame. A towering inferno enveloped the well and its children and stood ten, fifteen feet tall. Not spontaneous combustion, no; the fire started from outside the view of the window. The stream narrowed, and Daniel realized it was because the source was coming into frame.

A man in a fluorescent yellow hazmat suit walked into view, still training his flamethrower on the creatures. At first, they didn't respond to the heat, but then their bodies writhed and twisted, limbs and eyes emerging and then melting away. Daniel once again saw teeth and hair (and what looked like fingernails) suspended in the burning goo, even at this distance, before it liquified completely and sunk back into the earth. The creatures' screams sounded like Styrofoam burning.

BANG. The noise came from the front door. *BANG.* They were knocking down his door. *BANG.* It didn't take long. His door burst open and two men with battering rams rushed into his house. Two men with rifles came in after them, and then another man in a suit came in last.

"Agent Cohen," the man said. "I'm with the Bureau." Daniel didn't ask which one.

"Okay," he said.

"You killed them!" Mason screamed. He hid behind Daniel's leg and sobbed. "You killed the lil guys!"

"Are there any more on the premises?" Agent Cohen asked.

"There's one," Daniel said. "Somewhere. We don't know where."

"Okay," Agent Cohen said. This calmed Daniel for some reason. Agent Cohen turned to one of the armed men beside him. "Secure the basement."

"Copy," the man with the rifle said, and walked up to Daniel. "Where's the basement?"

"This way." Mason grabbed Daniel's pants leg and tried to stop him.

"What are you going to do?" Mason called out to Agent Cohen. The Agent paused for a second, considering his answer.

"We are attempting to contain the situation," he said. Then he turned around and walked out.

((((((((((o))))))))))

The man with the rifle cleared the basement. Mason's creature was unaccounted for. He stood in the center of the room and aimed his rifle at the stairs.

"You can sit," the man with the rifle said to them. "Somewhere behind me."

Daniel had covered the basement with tarps, now covered in dried goop. The basement was coated in a thick layer of crusted, creature excrement. He tried to lift the corner of one, but it was stuck to the floor beneath it. Flakes of dried ooze drifted lazily in the air. The tarps themselves were glued together, so Daniel had no choice but to sit on the goop-dust and try not to think about where Mason's creature might be.

The floor didn't seem to bother Mason. He took out his phone and started watching a live stream of one of the influencers walking through town, hugging their creature to their face.

"Mason, don't," Daniel said.

"It's fine, Dad."

"Okay," Daniel said.

"Catabolism is underway," the man with the rifle's walkie-talkie said. "Code black."

"What does that mean?" Daniel asked. He was interrupted by screams coming from upstairs. No, not upstairs. From Mason's phone. He looked at the screen and learned the meaning of catabolism.

Video of the woman from the first day. Ashley. No, Ashleighh. Two Hs. Eight hundred thousand viewers. She sat on the sidewalk, clutching the creature to her face. Screams sounded from off camera. Her creature started to change. Nubs grew from the goop and hugged Ashleighh's face. They grew into tendrils that gripped her skull.

"He's hugging me," Ashleighh said. "He must be so scared!"

The tendrils widened, and the creature softened, and suddenly Ashleighh's entire skull was encased in the goop. Now that the lil guy was viscous again, its skin became translucent again, like the goop had been straight from the bucket. Daniel could see Ashleighh screaming, but no sound escaped the goop.

Holes soon appeared in Ashleighh's face. Through the goop, he saw her skin melt away, the red muscle beneath twitching while Ashleighh tried to cry out. Daniel saw her eyes pop and dissolve, and then her eye sockets were just goop. Clumps of her hair floated through the ooze, separated from her exposed skull.

Ashleighh's face went slack; and that's when her hand finally dropped the camera. It landed face down on the concrete. Daniel saw all of this happen. Then he realized that Mason had too. Mason opened a menu on the side of the live stream and clicked on the hashtag #LILGUYS.

"Mason, don't," Daniel said. Mason didn't say anything, and Daniel didn't do anything to stop him.

On the screen was a man, lifting his shirt and aiming his phone at his stomach. One million viewers.

"What's happening?" the man yelled. His voice barely sounded human. The skin of his stomach rippled and bulged. Something was moving inside. Daniel wondered how the creature got inside of him. The camera panned up to the panicked man's face. His mouth was covered with goop.

The creature had gone down his throat. Now it wanted out. The camera pointed back down to the man's stomach and the bulges burst. Goop and thick rope poured out of where the skin split. The split grew bigger and then became an absence; the front of the man's torso was simply not there any longer. His lungs and ribs were exposed, and Daniel could see the man's heart beating before it stopped. Then he remembered that Mason could see too.

"Mason, don't," Daniel said. Mason didn't say anything, and Daniel didn't do anything to stop him. Mason clicked on the hashtag #LILGUYS again.

A stationary close up shot of a person's screaming face. One and a half million viewers. The bottom half of their jaw encased in goop. Their screams turned to gurgles, they clawed at their mouth and their jaw detached in their hands. They gurgled some more and dropped the drippy jaw. Hands reached for the camera and Daniel saw that they were covered in goop. Their fingernails detached, and their fingers started to separate. #LILGUYS.

Someone recorded a woman whose entire midsection was eaten away. One point eight million viewers. Her ribs and spine persisted; but all muscles and organs had been replaced by goop. Her spine folded and the top half of her body fell backward, hitting the pavement with a wet *splat*. In the background several immolations occurred. The woman's legs slumped to the ground. Three people were on fire, screaming. #LILGUYS.

A stationary shot in the middle of a street. Two and a half million viewers. There were eight distinct piles on the street that Daniel could see of goop and half digested body parts. A house was on fire. The piles started to move. They slopped towards each other and congregated in the middle of the street. They formed a massive orb of sludge that held all the disparate pieces of the beings it consumed within it. The orb slowly rolled out of frame. *Slosh. Sloosh. Slooooooosh.*

Mason turned off his phone. Only then did Daniel hear the sound of Mason crying.

"Dad," he said. "I miss Mom."

"Me too, bud," Daniel said. He put his hand on Mason's shoulder. "Me too."

((((((((((((o))))))))))))

Plop. Plop. Plop. The sound was coming from the stairs. The man with the rifle aimed.

"Get behind me," he told Mason and Daniel. They were already behind him. *Plop. Plop. Plop.* The creature rolled into view. It righted itself and aimed its motionless googly eyes at the man. Its little nubs pawed at the crusty ground and started to walk.

"Don't hurt him!" Mason yelled. The man with the rifle emptied his entire clip. Mason put his hands over his ears. Daniel put his hands over Mason's hands. The creature jiggled violently in place as it was riddled with bullet holes. *Click. Click.* The man with the rifle was out of ammo. The creature stared for a moment and then continued its slow walk towards him.

"Shit," he said. He poked the creature with the butt of his gun, trying to keep it at bay, but the goop absorbed the gun and continued its approach.

"Fuck," the man without a rifle said. It was pathetic how useless he was. The man went to kick the creature and the blob stuck to his foot. The creature started absorbing the man's boot. After that, the man without a rifle started to scream.

Daniel was frozen with fear. He missed Rae. She would know what to do.

Mason turned his phone screen on, aimed it at the screaming and now dissolving man in front of them, and started live-streaming.

ABOUT THE AUTHORS

KEEGAN is a writer, voice actor & filmmaker in Toronto. When he's not marathoning horror movies (join in on the festivities: @k33gan on instagram), he can be found playing roguelite deckbuilders, cheering on the Leafs, and throwing endless frisbees for his dog, Zamboni.

KAY HANIFEN (she/her) was born on a Friday the 13th and once lived for three months in a haunted castle. So, obviously, she had to become a horror writer. Her work has appeared in over fifty anthologies and magazines.

When she's not consuming pop culture with the voraciousness of a vampire at a 24-hour blood bank, you can usually find her with her black cats or at kayhanifenauthor.wordpress.com. Twitter: TheUnicornComi1

Instagram: <u>katharinehanifen/</u>

RAIN CORBYN is an autistic agender writer and narrator living in despair and the Catskills with their partner, dog, and bacteria waiting for us all to become meat milkshakes. More of their recent writing can be found in The Skull & Laurel Issue #1 (Tenebrous Press), There's No Escape (Inky Bones Press) and the benefit anthologies Howlin' For You and Tasteful. They narrate horror as themself, and romance/erotica as Richard Pendragon. Yes, they narrated the door erotica. And the Shrek smut. And the pillow porn. Please direct all complaints and outrage to @RainCorbyn on most socials.

JESSICA LUKE GARCIA (any pronouns) was raised in the rural borderlands of the American Midwest. They currently live in Las Palmas de Gran Canaria, Spain with their husband, Erik, and Antigonus, a retired feral cat.
They can be found online @10itemsorjess, and at <u>www. jessicalukegarcia.com</u>.

KYLA LUTZ got her start writing Lord of the Rings fanfiction at the tender age of nine and never really stopped. She lives in Ontario, Canada, with two cats and two pugs, and spends her spare time hiking the Canadian Shield and attempting to bake. Inspired by Kafka, Stoker, and Austen, her works are an eclectic mix of horror, romance, and the just plain weird.
She's never been published before.

RYAN MCANDREWS is a writer, actor, and comedian based in Los Angeles. His debut short horror story collection, The Darkling Stars, was recently self-published through Amazon. You can find him at ryanmcandrews.com, on IG @ ryn_mca, or on Bluesky @ ryanmcandrews.bsky.social

JOE KOCH writes literary horror and surrealist trash. Their books include The Wingspan of Severed Hands, Convulsive, Invaginies, and The Couvade, a 2019 Shirley Jackson Award finalist. His short works appear in Vastarien, Southwest Review, PseudoPod, Children of the New Flesh, The Mad Butterfly's Ball, and many others. Find Joe (He/They) at horrorsong.blog.

RORY G. is an essayist, educator, and horror writer based in Texas. Their short fiction has featured in British Fantasy Award-nominated anthology series The Book of Queer Saints (Medusa Haus 2023) and will feature in a forthcoming anthology centred around disability and neurodivergence in fantasy. Their nonfiction has featured in the Austin-American Statesman and Apocalypse Confidential.
You can find Rory online @gilhouligan on all platforms.

MARY SANCHE is a queer writer, illustrator & museum designer living in Canada, whose writing explores the union between science, art, & genre.
Read their work in Baffling Magazine, Heartlines Spec, and

Howls from the Scene of the Crime.

REBECCA (she/her) is a writer and editor from Ottawa, Ontario. Her short stories and poetry have been published in Augur, Strange Horizons, Bourbon Penn, Translunar Traveller's Lounge and other literary locations. She is Managing Editor at Heartlines Spec and was a Senior Editor at Apparition Lit (2017-2024). You can follow her online at @rebecca-b.bsky.social or jrlbennett.ca

JESSICA DOUTSAS (she/her) is a brand new writer, who is obsessed with Halloween, history, and pop culture. She lives in Toronto with her cats, Elvis and Birdie, and an aggressively large collection of books.
You can follow along with her writing and reading adventures on instagram and TikTok @JdoutsBookNook.

JF FOSTER (he/they) is a writer, musician and drag artist based in so-called Vancouver, BC. A voracious reader from youth, JF's journey with writing began during the lockdowns of 2020/21 as a way to cope with (among other things) missing in-person choirs and drag shows. His debut story, The Drag Mothers, was released in 2023 as part of the Demons & Death Drops anthology from Little Ghost Books. JF's favourite literary character is Lestat de Lioncourt from Anne Rice's Vampire Chronicles.

More information on JF and his work can be found on socials at @shesterrible_ .

ANDREW RIVAS (he/him) has written six books, including a crime thriller called EAT THE RICH and a memoir about being held illegally in a psych ward for seventeen days following a suicide attempt. He is a normal man that will continue writing weird and hyper-specific fiction until someone forces him to stop. He is 36 and lives in New York.

You can find him and his work at andrew-rivas.com or @andrewtrivas on twitter.

ABOUT THE EDITOR

LOR GISLASON (they/them) is an autistic non-binary homebody from Vancouver Island, Canada. Their articles have been featured on Hear Us Scream, Horror Obsessive and several upcoming anthologies. They edited the trans body horror anthology, Bound in Flesh, for Ghoulish Books. Their dream is to one day make an encyclopedia covering body horror films. Their novella, Inside Out, is available wherever goopy books are sold.

Follow them on Twitter @lorelli_ and BluSky @lormaggot

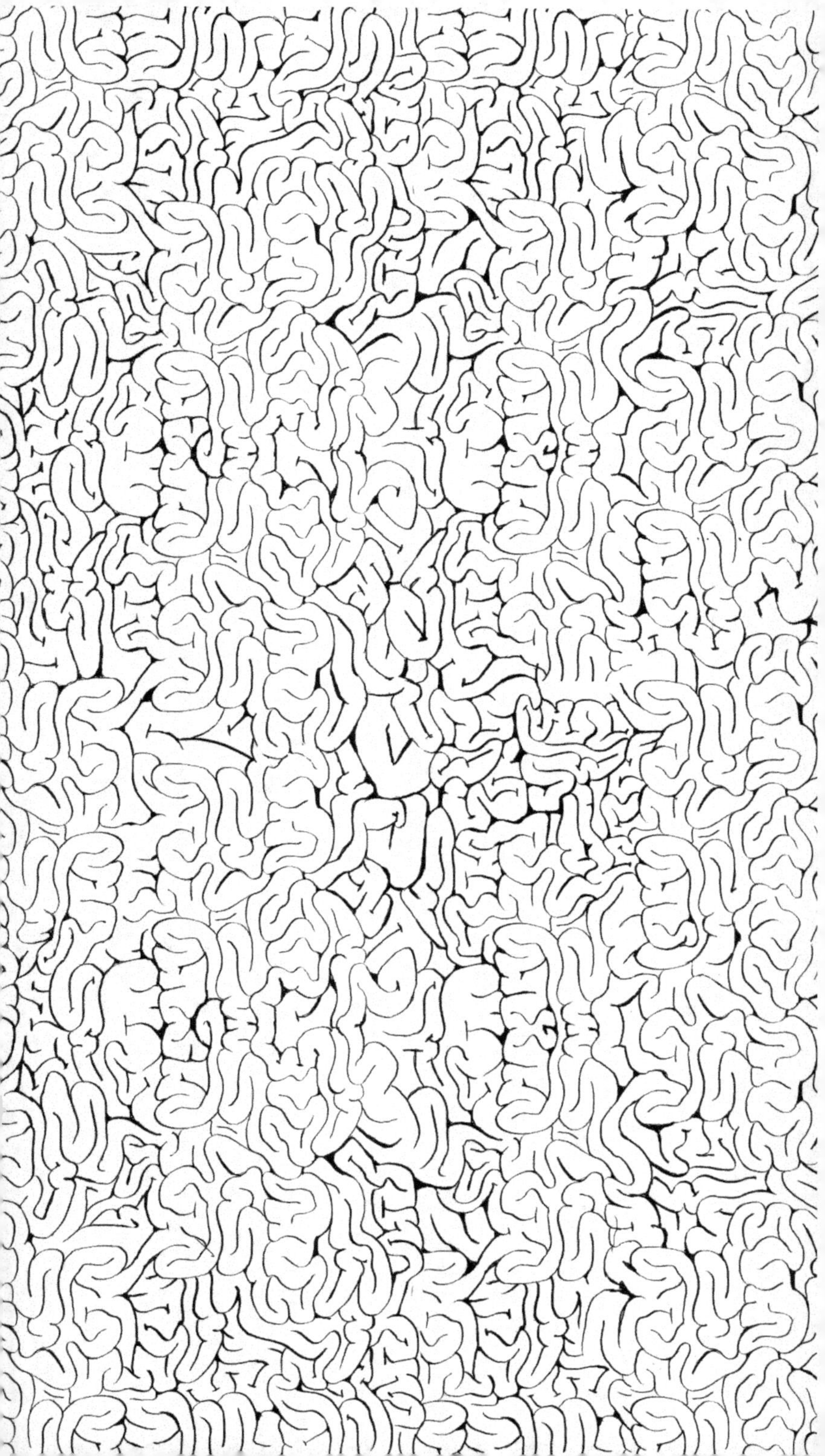